FEB 03 2020

D0091507

Carl Weber's Kingpins:

Harlem

NO LONGER PROPERTY OF
SEATTLE PUBLIC LIBRARY

FEB 0 3 2020

NO LONGER PROPERTY OF
SEATTLE PUBLIC LIBRARY

Carl Weber's Kingpins:

Harlem

C. N. Phillips

URBAN BOOKS

www.urbanbooks.net

Urban Books, LLC
300 Farmingdale Road, N.Y.-Route 109
Farmingdale, NY 11735

Carl Weber's Kingpins: Harlem

Copyright © 2020 C. N. Phillips

All rights reserved. No part of this book may be repro-
duced in any form or by any means without prior consent
of the Publisher, except brief quotes used in reviews.

ISBN 13: 978-1-893196-02-5
ISBN 10: 1-893196-02-X

First Trade Paperback Printing February 2020
Printed in the United States of America

10 9 8 7 6 5 4 3 2 1

*This is a work of fiction. Any references or similarities
to actual events, real people, living or dead, or to real
locales are intended to give the novel a sense of reality.
Any similarity in other names, characters, places, and
incidents is entirely coincidental.*

Distributed by Kensington Publishing Corp.
Submit Orders to:
Customer Service
400 Hahn Road
Westminster, MD 21157-4627
Phone: 1-800-733-3000
Fax: 1-800-659-2436

Carl Weber's Kingpins:

Harlem

by

C. N. Phillips

Dedication

This book is dedicated to Nipsey Hussle. I love you forever, King. I will forever thank God that He guided me to your words. I was a new mom when I first heard your voice all those years ago . . . You made me believe that I could really build a good life for my daughter. For us. I will always be grateful for that. I will always appreciate you for helping me pull myself back up after those long nights. This dream of mine is one that nobody supported, but when I heard your words, it made me okay with being on this marathon by myself. *"This life is short; let's make it worth it, nigga. We all so far from perfect, nigga. The cameras rollin', no rehearsals, nigga. Plus scared money never made a fuckin' purchase, nigga."* You were and will always be great. Nobody can take that away from you. You were more than an artist to me. You touched my soul, and for that, you will be with me forever. RIP to the greatest!

"The path to success is to take massive, determined actions."

—Tony Robbins

Prologue

September 1996

"Touch me, tease me. Feel me and caress me. Hold on tight and don't let go. Baby, I'm about to explode!"

Case's voice boomed from a loudspeaker and into the hot New York air. The smell of barbecue and sound of laughter filled the backyard of Arnold "Sunny" Walker's three-story home. Most hustlers wouldn't take a day off, but for Sunny, Sundays were a day for family to get together and mingle. He'd built the biggest cocaine operation Harlem had ever seen, and he wanted to reap what he'd sown. He stood over the grill, flipping burgers in a pair of sneakers, shorts, and silk floral button-up that was open at the top. The thick gold chain on his neck matched the Rolex on his wrist, and both glistened in the sunlight. Sunny was what the women called one pretty-ass man because he was just that handsome. He had soft hazelnut eyes with long eyelashes, full lips, a strong jaw structure, and kept his hair cut in a short high-top fade. His good looks mixed with his light skin was what always made the girls go crazy. Sunny's looks were also why some people thought he was soft, but he liked that. It gave him a reason to unleash the beast within him; however, this wasn't one of those times. He was enjoying the family time and watching while his children swam in the pool with their cousins. The women and elder folks were sitting at the bench tables chatting while his boys stood around the grill with ice-cold beers in their hands.

"Man, you need some help with them burgers? I don't want no pink in my shit!"

Sunny grinned at the sound of his right-hand man, Kyan's, voice. The two had been in it since they were waddling in diapers and carrying bottles everywhere. "Day" and "Night" was what they were called growing up, and not just because Sunny was high yellow and Kyan was chocolate. No, it was deeper than that. Sunny and Kyan each had a personality that balanced the other. Sunny could admit that his operation wouldn't be nearly as successful without Kyan's muscle, nor would Kyan be eating as well as he was without Sunny's brain. Both men were tall, but Kyan was taller and was more muscular. He too was a handsome man who wore his hair cut low so that his waves busted out. That day, he wore a baseball cap to the back and a baseball jersey completely unbuttoned.

"Nigga, you better shut ya ass up before I 'accidently' leave some pink in ya burger," Sunny said, waving the spatula at him. "Gon' be callin' me tomorrow talkin' 'bout 'Dog, I can't put in no work today. I'm on the toilet.'"

"You would do me like that, God?"

"You the one playin' like a nigga doesn't get busy on the grill," Sunny said with a laugh.

"Yeah, Kyan, you over here playin' my boy," their friend Cross piped up. "You know the food is the top reason I make sure I'm here on time every Sunday!"

Sunny nodded his head and dapped up Cross.

"Yeah, nigga," he said, looking back at Kyan. "How my soldiers hype me, but my right hand don't?"

"'Cause I'm already at the cool table. I don't gotta dick ride ya ugly ass!"

"Yeah, whatever," Sunny told him and closed the grill so the burgers could cook a little longer. "Aye, Cross, watch the grill. I gotta holla at my mans for a second."

"Word," Cross answered and took the spatula.

"Let's go in the house for a second," Sunny said and nodded toward the patio slide door.

Before he took a step, Sunny felt a cold, wet hand grab his arm. When he looked down, he saw his 8-year-old daughter, Mariah, looking up at him with a towel wrapped around her body.

"Daddy, is the food done? I'm starving!"

"Not yet, baby, but if you need somethin' in ya stomach right away, go ask Mommy for some chips."

"OK, and, Daddy?"

"Yes, baby?"

"Man Man keeps pinching our legs under water! He's pissing me off!"

"Aye! Watch ya mouth," Sunny said, gently popping Mariah's lips. "Don't speak like that. You're only a kid, remember? And tell ya brother I said stop pinching legs, or I'ma pinch him, a'ight?"

"OK, Daddy," Mariah said and ran back to the pool instead of to the table with the chips.

"Kids," he said, shaking his head. "Come on, Ky, before another one of these crumb snatchers harasses me for some eats again."

He slid the patio door behind him and led Kyan into the basement of his lavish home. Sunny had to admit, his wife, Keisha, had outdone herself when she decorated their house. She was an interior decorator, and their home was her big project, and every time Sunny walked through it, he felt like a king. She'd done the basement specifically for him. It was his man cave, complete with a bar and a pool table. Sunny went behind the bar and poured two glasses of Rémy Martin on the rocks. Kyan sat on a bar stool across from him and picked up his glass.

"What's good, boss?" Kyan asked, swiveling the liquid around in the cup.

"The streets are talkin', and that ain't good," Sunny said, giving Kyan a look before taking a gulp of his drink.

"The streets are always talkin', so you're gonna have to be a little more specific with that one."

"They're talkin' about that cat we ran out of town a few weeks back."

"Kameron?"

"Yeah, that's the one."

"Well, what can they be sayin' about that nigga that has ya drawers in a frenzy? He came here tryin' to expand. We said no and kicked him out of our territory. That's how this shit usually goes."

"Yeah, I know, but Cross told me that he's talkin' retaliation."

"Retaliation for what? We ain't even do them niggas how we usually do niggas movin' in on our turf. We let them go. That nigga Cross be sayin' anything, man. I wouldn't even pay it no mind."

"You ain't think they went a little too peacefully?" Sunny asked. "I mean, why even ruffle the birds' feathers in the first place if you don't care about the outcome?"

To that, Kyan just clenched his jaws. He set the glass he was holding down on the bar and leaned back in his seat. From where Sunny stood, he could tell his boy's head was reeling just by the expression on his face. Or maybe he thought that because his own mind was going fifty miles a second. Kameron was a few years older than Kyan and him, but his operation hadn't quite taken flight yet. To do that, he needed Sunny. What he'd brought to the table was something more than a cocaine empire. He *was proposing that they take over every market, and that included marijuana and pills. It was something to think about, and the way Kameron was talking, it was clear that he had a plan, but Sunny could tell that Kameron was the type of man that didn't like not being in charge. There was something about the look in his eyes that couldn't be trusted, and not only that, Sunny knew he had a great thing going. Downfall only came to the greedy man, and for now, he had all that he needed. He didn't want to risk adding more eyes, ears, and hands to his pot. So he declined Kameron's offer and told him in so many words to make sure he stayed out of Harlem with his work.*

"You worried?"

"Nah, not worried. Cautious. Men like Kameron want to take over the world and never give up this game. Those are the ones you have to look out for. The ones who want to live like this forever."

"I mean, I don't know about you, but I could be on top forever," Kyan said with a shrug of his shoulders.

"I feel that, and I definitely want to be on top forever. But my forever doesn't involve being a kingpin."

"What, you gonna go legit and become some top chef or some shit?"

"Maybe," Sunny grinned. "Or maybe I'll buy some more property and invest, but all I know is that in order to ensure I see that future, I have to dot all my i's and cross all of my t's, starting with Kameron."

"I feel it. We have a few more years to put in before we can call it quits, though."

"Word," Sunny said and raised his glass. "To our future."

"Our future," Kyan said, lifting his glass and putting it to his lips.

The men had barely swallowed a drop when they heard a sound that made both of their hearts drop.

Boom! Boom! Boom! Boom!

The gunshots caught the two of them off guard, and when they didn't stop, Sunny knew they weren't celebratory rounds. He quickly pulled his 9-millimeter pistol from his waist and rushed to the patio door with Kyan closely behind. He peered outside the window and saw all of his men dropping one by one like flies. He couldn't get eyes on the shooters, but when he saw his children cowering under a bench, Sunny knew it was time to be about action. When he slid the door open and stepped outside, the glass on the patio door instantly was shot out.

"There he go!" he heard a voice shout out. "Lay that nigga down!"

He and Kyan dropped to the ground and rolled out of the way. Looking around the large backyard, he saw many of his family members on the ground bleeding out, including Keisha. She was holding her stomach and trying to crawl to the kids, but a man was standing over her with a gun pointed at her head.

"Keisha!" Sunny yelled and tried to aim his gun, but the grill was in the way of his shot.

Boom!

Kyan fired his weapon, and his bullet caught the man standing over Keisha in the temple. Sunny began firing shots at the other two men who had materialized standing near the entrance to his backyard. His guests who weren't already on the ground were screaming and scrambling, trying to get out of that backyard. Little did they know, they were making their survival rate plummet. Their bodies kept getting in the way of bullets, and they were dropping like flies. Sunny saw Cross's lifeless body by the grill and figured that the men must have caught him off guard. Kyan and Sunny seemed to be the last ones left, and they were holding their own.

"Daddy!"

Sunny saw Mariah emerge from under a table, and he tried to shout for her to stay there, but it was too late. She saw where he was taking cover and decided to run toward him.

"Mariah, no, baby!" he yelled, but it was too late.

She never saw the bullet that caught her in the back of the head. She dropped dead instantly, and Sunny's eyes grew as big as saucers. The gun in his hand wavered after watching his only daughter get gunned down in front of him.

"Mariah!" he shouted, and hot tears fell down his face.

"Kameron sends his love!" One of the men shouted and headed toward the spot Mariah had just left.

Sunny's son was still there under the table hiding with his hands covering his head. Sunny tried to aim for the man after him, but there was no use. Every shot he made missed, and the incoming fire at him made it almost impossible to make a move. Sunny's clip was empty, and he was out of ammunition. He had no other choice; he had to get to his son somehow.

"Cover me," he told Kyan and took off toward his son just as the man wearing all black reached him.

Sunny ran the five feet to his terrified child. He put his body in front of him and looked into the eyes of his enemy. He saw humor in them, as if it had all been just a game.

"Kameron said you'd be tougher than this," the man said.

He wore no mask, and that meant there were to be no witnesses that day. He looked to be the same age as Sunny, yet his eyes had the look of a man who had never known happiness. He raised his gun at Sunny and applied his finger on the trigger.

"What do you want? Whatever he's payin' you, I can double it," Sunny heard himself plead.

"Loyalty don't work like that," the young man said and cocked his gun. "I hope ya son was worth savin'."

Boom!

The bullet caught Sunny in the side of his forehead, and he felt a piercing pain when his neck snapped back. His vision went black, but not before he saw the man standing over him get gunned down.

Chapter 1

"One finds limits by pushing them."
—Herbert Simon

2019

Klax Turner hated when things didn't go as planned. When it came to business, he was a very particular man. He liked things to go smoothly so that they didn't have to get ugly. But it seemed that somebody was dead set on forcing his hand. In a short period of time, someone had ordered hits on two of Klax's stash spots. The gunmen didn't make it into Harlem; nobody ever made it into Harlem. And if they did, they didn't make it very far. It was too easy to tell if you didn't belong there. However, over $100,000 of cash and cocaine were stolen from a storage unit in the Bronx. There was only one other person who knew about the storage unit, and that was the person who was in charge of watching it. Big Tony.

Big Tony had worked for Klax's father, Kameron Turner, before his untimely death. He was ten years older than Klax and had worked his way up in rank during his service. He'd gone from running errands to running every corner in the Bronx. There had never been a problem for years, and Big Tony was a hardworking man, but something was off. Klax was supposed to be in a meeting early that morning for a property that he was about to acquire, but instead, he was on his way to figure out why Big Tony had slacked at his post. He drove his silver G-Wagen through the morning New York traffic until he finally made it to his destination. The hairs on the back of his neck stood up when he parked his car in Big Tony's driveway. Klax smoothed down the Saint Laurent button-up he was wearing as he looked around the neighborhood. The large houses were about twenty feet away from each other, and it seemed as if everyone had already left for the morning. Other than the cold wind blowing and a few cars pulling out of their driveways, it was quiet. Klax stepped out of the truck and went to the front door of the house.

Ding, dong!

After Klax rang the doorbell, Ransom, one of Big Tony's workers, opened the door. He stood tall but straightened up even more when he saw Klax. He nodded his head in respect and backed out of the way so that Klax could enter.

"Where's your boss?" Klax asked, standing in the foyer of the house.

"He's in the back. Follow me," Ransom said and started to walk, assuming Klax would follow.

"How about you tell him to meet me in the front room," Klax suggested and pointed at the all-white room to the right of them. "I'll wait."

"Yes sir," Ransom said and left.

Klax didn't bother looking around at anything that wasn't obvious to the eye in the house. He walked, as if he owned the place, to the white couch in the sitting room and patiently waited. Big Tony knew that he hated waiting, so it was a good thing he showed his face soon after.

"Klax!" Big Tony said loudly entering the room resembling Barney in the purple crewneck shirt he wore.

Klax stood up to quickly shake Big Tony's hand and pull him into an embrace. Then he retook his seat while Big Tony sat in a chair across from him. Goons positioned themselves in a half circle behind Big Tony's seat and stood ready in case anything happened.

"We usually only have to meet face-to-face once a month, Tony," Klax said. "There's something wrong with this picture."

"Trust me, Klax. I have had motherfuckas scouring the streets looking for the sons of bitches that stole from you."

"Can you run by me exactly what happened again?"

"I think somebody followed me when I went to go check on the storage, because the day it happened, I had just left from there."

"Is that right?" Klax said, leaning back in his seat.

"Yeah, man," Big Tony said sincerely. "I'm going to get your shit back on everything. And when I catch whoever it is, they're gonna pay."

"I hope so," Klax said, looking Big Tony in the eye. "And just so we're on the same page, exactly how are you going to make them pay for stealing from me?"

"I'm going to chain his ankle to the back of my truck and go for a little ride," Big Tony said without missing a beat.

"I like that," Klax said with an approving nod. "Get on it."

He stood up from his seat like he was about to leave, but stopped abruptly like he forgot something.

"You good, G?" Big Tony asked.

"Yeah, I just almost completely forgot what I came here for. Ransom, will you go to my trunk and bring me what's inside," Klax asked, and without hesitation, Ransom went outside to Klax's car. "I have a package for you. I like you, Tony; you're ambitious. You want more work, don't you?"

"More work?" Big Tony inquired, and a happy smile spread across his face. "Boss, I just got promoted, and we're pushing more keys a week than we should already."

"Can't handle it?"

"Hell yeah, I can handle it. I just am gonna need some more territory. You know I've been asking you about Harlem for a long time now."

"And the answer will be the same every time. The shit I have going in Harlem is untouchable right now, but it doesn't surprise me that you bring up Harlem right now."

"And why is that?" Big Tony said evenly.

At that time, Big Tony's goon had returned with what Klax had sent him outside to get. He wore a shocked look on his face because what they all assumed was a real package wasn't at all. Half walking and half being dragged by the goon was a man who was sporting two swollen eyes and a bloodied face. His mouth was covered with duct tape, and his wrists were tied together. The second the man saw Klax. He bucked and tried to run away, but couldn't. Klax glanced casually at him and then turned back to Big Tony, who was wearing an expression of shock on his face.

"Drop him right here," Klax said, pointing at a spot near his feet.

The goon did as he was told and went back to his post. The man on the ground cowered and kept his eyes on the floor he was staining with his blood. Klax fought the urge to kick him in the side of his face, but only because he needed him conscious.

"W-what's going on here?" Big Tony finally said after the surprise wore off. "You can't just be pulling niggas out of your trunk in front of my house!"

"Why can't I?" Klax asked. "I think you've forgotten who I am, haven't you?"

"Nah, Klax," Big Tony said with his eyes shifting from Klax to the man on the ground in front of him.

"I think you have. You know, when you first told me about the robbery, I thought to myself, 'This shit had to have been plotted.' But who could be targeting me?"

"Maybe it was those boys from upstate," Big Tony offered. "Raul and them. You know they feel as if you stole their clientele."

"I thought that too at first, but Raul makes too much money with my product; that, and the fact that he wouldn't stand a fighting chance. He would never step to me. So, the more I thought about it, I concluded that because there were two hits, there is definitely someone gunning for me. But this Bronx hit was too specific. Nobody knew about that storage . . . except you."

"Boss, are you saying I would rob you?"

"I'm saying that the storage wasn't the target. You were. The things taken from me were just the icing on the cake."

"You can't really think I would lie to you, Klax. Me and your old man go way back in the day!"

"I didn't have to. Our friend here told me everything that I needed to know," Klax said gesturing to the man on the ground. "You may not recognize him with all those knots on his head."

Big Tony stared hard at the man on the ground, and Klax watched him suddenly recognize the man.

"Yeah, I thought he would be familiar to you," Klax said. "My people caught him bragging around the city about the big lick he'd just hit. They brought him to me, and you wouldn't believe the song this little birdie sang. Now, tell me if this is fact or fiction, a'ight? So, this nigga here tells me that he followed you to the storage to offer you a deal, not to rob me. He said that he told you if you helped his boss take me down, then you could run the Bronx *and* Harlem. He said that you gave them my money and drugs to show 'good faith.'"

Big Tony didn't say anything; instead, he just glared at Klax when he continued speaking. "I'll take your silence as I'm right. A'ight. But just tell me this, you really gave this nigga my shit to show good faith?"

"Fuck you," Big Tony finally said, realizing his game was blown. "I don't know what Kam was thinking of leaving his empire to you anyway. You ain't shit but a little boy in this game, Klax. Give it up. It's time for someone new to run the game."

"And I take it that someone is you?" Klax asked, genuinely amused.

"Yeah, nigga!" Big Tony's deep voice said loudly. "I don't know why you're sitting over there thinking shit is funny. I've been in the game since you were still counting with your fingers. I think it's about time *I* run the streets. You come in here tryna make me shake in my Louboutins with some nigga you beat up like I'm supposed to be scared or something. All you niggas have shown me is that you're weak and stupid. Now *you* tell *me* something, Klax. Did you *really* think you could come in here alone and just walk out?" Big Tony's lips spread into a menacing smile, and he gave a hearty laugh as he motioned to his goons. "Kill this nigga."

He leaned back and waited to hear the gunshots that Klax knew never were going to come. When Big Tony realized that Klax wasn't lying in a pool of his own blood, he turned his head and was met with another surprise. He had five guns pointed at him, and that caused him to jump up from his seat, angry.

"What the fuck is this?" he shouted at them. "Where is your loyalty? You work for *me!*"

"And *you* work for *me*. Which means *they* work for *me* too," Klax reminded Big Tony. "They would never raise their guns to me. Now, *that's* loyalty. Something that you don't have. And because of that, you've been discharged from your position."

"Nigga, you can't discharge me! I built the Bronx! Can't nobody run this shit like me—"

Pfft!

Big Tony was cut short when his head suddenly snapped viciously back. The bullet from Klax's gun caught him in the middle of the forehead. The man on the floor jumped hard when Big Tony's brains sprayed on his furniture, and his body fell to the ground. He was dead.

"I trust that one of you will get this cleaned up," Klax said to the goons, who nodded quickly. "Good."

Klax ignored Big Tony's dead body and knelt in front of the terrified man. He snatched the duct tape from his mouth and dropped it on the floor. The man had had so much heart when he was first snatched up. It took awhile to break him down, but soon, he found out that underneath Klax's charming exterior, there was a monster living inside. He told Klax everything he needed to know except one thing.

"Who sent you?" Klax demanded.

"I already told you," the man breathed. "I can't tell you."

"That's not an answer. You have three seconds to tell me who sent you, or else you end up like our friend here."

"I told you as much as I can," the man said and stared Klax in the eyes. He held the look of a man who had already accepted death. "I'd rather go back in a box than go back with breath in my lungs. There ain't shit you can do to me that will compare to what *he'll* do to me. So just kill me. I ain't telling you shit el—"

Pfft!

The bullet from Klax's gun was lodged in his skull before he finished speaking. His chin dropped to his chest, and his eyes closed. Klax sighed and shook his head in front of the dead man. Whoever he worked for put a fear in his heart that not even Klax could scare away. Not only that, but whoever it was had gone to great lengths to get to him. He'd found the weakest link in Klax's camp, and that couldn't have been easy. That let Klax know that he was being watched.

"Nobody comes in or out of here until this shit is cleaned up," Klax told Ransom. "Also, until I appoint someone new, you're in charge of shit over here. You cool with that?"

"Yeah, I'm cool with it," Ransom said, looking down at Big Tony's body. "As long as I don't end up like him."

"If you make better decisions than him, you won't," Klax told him and made his way to the door.

When Klax got back into his car, the hairs on his neck stood up again. That time, not in anticipation of cracking down on someone who crossed him, but because he didn't know who was calling plays in his city. He also couldn't help but wonder what his father would say about all that had just happened. He would have been livid at the robbery, but he would have been angrier at the attempt on Harlem. Kameron Turner wouldn't stand for the disrespect on his own turf, so Klax knew exactly what he would say.

"I know, I know," he said to himself as he pulled out of the long driveway. "I need to tighten up."

Chapter 2

"It all comes down to the last person you think of at night. That's where your heart is."

—Anonymous

Kleigh

"Kleigh, when are you going to settle down and find someone to love you?"

Kleigh Turner rolled her eyes from where she lay on her queen-sized, silver sleigh bed. She was on her stomach, painting her nails a dazzling hot pink while her best friend, Bahli Samuels, sat at a vanity a few feet away from the bed. Bahli's face was an inch away from the mirror as she went over her eyebrows for what seemed like the tenth time.

"It's going to take a special kind of man to love me," Kleigh said, admiring the paint job she'd done by holding her hand up in the air.

"Well, maybe if you gave someone a chance, you would know if they were that special man! You don't even let anybody close to you."

Bahli, finally satisfied with her makeup, came and sat on the edge of Kleigh's bed. She was a beautiful girl with a mocha-brown complexion and thick, black hair that she kept tucked away under bundles of weave. She had a round face, big lips, and wide set, pretty, light brown eyes.

Bahli was nowhere near petite. She was a shapely young woman with a nice-sized rear end to match her plump chest. Her teeth shined due to the braces on them, but they just accented her vibrant smile. Her acrylic nails tapped the vanity in an annoyed fashion as she gave Kleigh a look waiting for her answer. If anybody knew Kleigh Turner, it was her. They'd been best friends since the first grade and looked at each other as sisters.

Kleigh returned Bahli's eye roll and sat up as well. At age 25, she had filled out quite nicely. Her C-cup breasts seemed so much bigger since her stomach was so flat. Her hips were naturally wide, and her big butt was round with a cuff. She was the epitome of what it meant to be "slim thick," and she had a pretty face to go along with all of her other attributes. On her oval-shaped head, she wore her hair natural in long, kinky curls. Her cheekbones were defined and raised high whenever she was happy or excited about something.

"All these niggas wanna do is fuck, and you know that. I don't even want to waste my time on any of them."

"Girl, you don't know that!"

"What's the point of letting somebody get close to me if they run off once they find out who my brother is?"

"True," Bahli said with a frown. "I forgot about that part."

Kleigh sighed at her best friend and just shook her head. She was starting to believe that there was no such thing as a happily ever after for her if Klax was in the picture. She loved her big brother, but he was the wall that wouldn't come down in her life. Ever since their father passed away, Klax made it his duty to be her provider and protector. She felt blessed—and smothered—at the same time. She loved how her brother loved her, but it was a hindrance at the same time. Sometimes, she felt that she had to *try* just to be normal. Every move she made was watched; every decision she made was scrutinized. She couldn't imagine bringing a man into that equation because no matter who he was, he would never measure up in Klax's eyes.

"Yeah, of course, you would forget. You're not the one with him as a brother," Kleigh told her with a sigh.

She got up from the bed and walked to the large window in her bedroom. Moving one of the white drapes to the side, she peered down to the street below. As always, one of Klax's goons was posted up outside of her condo, and she groaned loudly.

"This is the shit I be talkin' about!"

"Who is it this time? Butta or Drop?"

"From the looks of the new Benz, it has to be Drop," Kleigh answered.

"I need to fuck with *him*. He stays in a new car."

"That's why they call him Drop. He's been like that since he and Klax were younger," Kleigh let out a big breath. "I don't understand why Klax still treats me like a damn kid! Every time I turn around, I see one of his ugly-ass minions. It's starting to get on my nerves."

"Starting to? I think that's an understatement."

"I'm 25, and he's still clocking my every move."

"I get you, baby; trust me, I do. But on the real? You're the little sister of the head honcho of Harlem, and *that* makes you a princess. Don't go acting naive now. You know *exactly* why he keeps you on lock."

"I know who my big brother is, but I can handle myself. I'm not some defenseless little girl," Kleigh said and stepped away from the window. "I need some fresh air. Let's get out."

"Buuuut . . . It's Thursday," Bahli raised her perfectly arched eyebrow and looked skeptically at her friend.

"So? How long has it been since we went dancing?"

"Almost a month." Bahli pretended to think with a finger to her lips. "Because the last time we went out, some wild niggas shot the club up!"

"Stop being so dramatic. Find something in my closet. It's only about to be ten o'clock, and you know what that means. The night is still young!"

"The only way I'm going out with you is if you let me wear that black Dior dress with the back cut completely out." Bahli crossed her arms to let Kleigh know she was serious.

"How about not? I haven't even popped the tag on that yet!"

"I know," Bahli grinned mischievously. "And after I do, that means you won't want it back. That's my condition if you want my fine ass to step out with you tonight."

"You ain't right."

"How badly do you want me to go with you?"

"What kind of friend are you?"

"The kind that comes with a price."

"Whatever, heffa. Grab the damn dress. It's—"

"Hanging on the back of the closet door." Bahli jumped up and almost skipped to the closet. She snatched it down from the hanger and held it up to herself, staring at her reflection in the full-length mirror at the back of the closet. "I've been eyeing this dress since you got it in the mail!"

Kleigh watched Bahli admiring the fabric of the dress in her huge closet, wondering why the only designer that ever graced Bahli's body was never owned by her. Kleigh knew her friend made good money at her job. She was the assistant to one of the highest-paid lawyers in New York. It was obvious that Bahli had expensive taste, but she would settle for shopping out of regular, inexpensive department stores.

"You know you were with me when I ordered that dress, right? Why didn't you get your own?"

Kleigh entered the closet too and began to sift through what seemed like a ton of clothing in search of something to wear. Most of the items still had tags on them because she forgot they were there. She had really wanted to step out in the Dior dress, but she also didn't want to move around the city alone that night. So, she was willing to make the trade.

"Because that dress was almost $4,000, and not all of us have a wealthy big brother who covers all of our expenses. I still have to pay rent for my own spot on top of a car note, and all of the shit that comes with those things."

"Even if I didn't have a big brother that looks out the way Klax does, I would still have everything that I want. It costs to be the boss, LeeLee. Don't sit up here and act like I don't make my own money from my own business."

"A business that Klax gave you the startup money for."

"Startup money that I paid back in under a year," Kleigh whipped around and placed her hand on her hip. "You sound a little salty over there. You act like I didn't offer you a position to work for me. You turned it down because you didn't want to work *for* me."

"Because your ass is bossy!" Bahli said and grinned. "You know damn well we would bump heads every day if I were your employee!"

"You have a point there," Kleigh said and returned her smile. "I didn't mean what I said about ordering the dress to come out like that. You're my girl, and you know I got you through whatever. You want me to have Klax send some of his goons up to Mr. Bailor's firm and threaten him into giving you a raise?"

"Kleigh!" Bahli almost choked from laughing so hard. "You would scare that poor white man to death! No, I don't want you to do that. I make good money; it's just that everything in New York is so expensive!"

"OK, then," Kleigh shrugged, still thumbing through her clothes. "That was the first offer, which means you can't decline the second. I'm paying your bills for six months so you can stack up."

"Kleigh—"

"I'm not taking no for an answer. Business at the bakery is booming. We were on the Food Network last month! Plus, what's the point of being paid if you can't help your best friend out? Now, let's go shake our asses like we don't have any sense!"

She'd settled on a long-sleeved, deep wine-colored bodysuit with a deep V cut at the bosom, a pair of sexy distressed boyfriend jeans, and her new pair of black Christian Louboutin booties. From the top shelf, she snatched down a silver diamond-studded clutch for Bahli and a small black Gucci shoulder bag with a long gold chain strap for herself.

"You spoil me," Bahli said grinning as she admired the clutch.

"Yeah, yeah," Kleigh said, sending an air kiss her way. "You can go get in the shower first. I'm about to put on a quick face before we head out."

It was another hour before the girls were in Kleigh's 2018 dark purple Dodge Charger. She could have taken her pink BMW M5, but that meant Drop would have seen her whipping out of the parking garage. Which also meant he would have followed her to wherever she was at and probably called for backup, just in case. Just once, Kleigh wanted to be normal, like the other women her age. That was why she purchased the Charger without her brother ever knowing about it. She only took it out for a spin when she wanted to be real low-key, and that night was one of those times. When Kleigh pulled out of the parking garage and drove past Drop, she was pleased to see that he wasn't paying them any attention. He was busy looking down, probably scrolling on his phone. The second they made it past the Mercedes-Benz, Kleigh felt a wave of relief wash over her.

"That nigga was probably in there beating his meat," Bahli joked and then laughed.

"He can do whatever he wants as long as he thinks I'm still at home," Kleigh said and turned the music up.

They were in the clear, and the only thing on her mind was dipping low and shaking all that she had behind her at the new club, Diamonds. She'd heard so much about it, and it had been too long since she'd had a good time, and she was determined to make that one for the books.

Chapter 3

"Wisdom consists of the anticipation of consequences."
—Norman Cousins

Klax

"You sure the person you looking for is going to be up in here tonight?"

The sound of guns clicking and being loaded could be heard over the muffled sound of hip-hop music inside of the basement of Klax's new club, Diamonds. He stood beside one of his most trusted generals, Dame, watching as five of his young soldiers prepared for war. Dame was a cat originally from the West Coast. He was of average height, stocky, a dark-skinned man with a brush cut and stayed laced in nothing but designer. The only facial hair he had was a thin mustache. Other than that, he kept his baby face clean cut. Klax nodded his head at Dame's question.

"I laid the bread crumbs in hopes that whoever ordered those hits would follow. You heard about what I had to do to Big Tony yesterday. And the other cat never made it back to report anything because I had his body laid out in the street. That shit made the news."

"You think whoever the motherfucka is watches the news?"

"He wouldn't have to. This is New York. Word of mouth *is* the news. Same as the grand opening to this club. What better way to disrespect me than show up at my new spot?" Klax answered and looked up at the ceiling. "Even if the nigga ain't here to make noise, he'll be here. If I were him, I would be."

His heart bled for the innocent people that might get caught in the cross fire, and he knew the Feds would be sniffing around his nightclub, Diamonds, after tonight. However, one thing he didn't tolerate was disrespect, and he would cut off his own hand one million times before he allowed it in his own city. He hoped to lure his enemy out into an even level playing field; after all, a fight was no fun when the opponent was a phantom. He gave his young goons a head nod, letting them know that it was time for them to head up to the main floor of the building. They were under strict orders to blend in until they spotted their mark, and even then, Klax wanted whoever he was alive.

Klax smoothed out the sleeves of his beige Moncler jacket before rubbing his hands together. He had to admit, his matching red Gucci loafers set his whole outfit off. His light-skinned complexion made the natural auburn-colored hair on his head pop out. He liked to keep it cut in a low taper fade with a surgical line. Klax was a tall man at six foot three, muscular with broad shoulders, and tattoos that covered his neck and went down his arms and chest. The amber-colored eyes he had were a gift from his great-great-grandfather, and they apparently always skipped a few generations. He tucked his gun into his jeans. He felt as if he'd made the people wait long enough. It was time to show his face in the club. As he made his way to the stairwell, the gold chains on his neck clinked together. He had heard somewhere recently that real money was silent. That men with real wealth didn't rock designers or chains. That was all noise to Klax. Those people must have forgotten that they descended from a land where men proudly wore their wealth on their necks, wrists, ears, and even in their lips like the kings they were. And Klax was just that: a king. His jewels would gleam wherever he was, and he dared anyone to try to take them.

"If he outs himself, I want everyone that came with him dead," Klax said to Dame who was climbing the stairs beside him. "When the Feds come poking their noses around here, tell them that some niggas were fighting over a female, and it escalated."

"Got it," Dame nodded. "What about security footage?"

"We're going to tell them that our cameras have been down for a week. The wiring in the building was fried in that power surge last week, which was why we hired extra security so that these kinds of things wouldn't happen."

"And *that*, my guy, is why *you're* the king. Now, let's go find this weird-ass nigga."

They exited the basement and entered the club through the kitchen. It was almost midnight, so the cooks were bustling around trying to get the last-minute wing orders in before they shut it all down. None seemed shocked to see Klax and Dame appear out of nowhere, but they were sure to clear the walkway. It smelled delicious, and Klax couldn't help himself.

"Aye, make me twelve Jerk wings with a side of fries," he said over his shoulder to one of the cooks. "Take it back to my office."

They kept it moving until they had reached the main VIP section. Like a ruler eyeing his kingdom, Klax looked over the club. It was packed, and there wasn't one person on the dance floor who wasn't moving to the loud music. Klax had hired the hottest DJ in the city, a DJ to work for him exclusively, and it had proved to be a power move. He glanced across the club for a second before he felt a hand on his shoulder.

"The nigga of the hour has finally chosen to bless us with his presence!"

Klax grinned when he heard the voice. Turning around, he found himself face-to-face with Adonis, the man who had been his best friend since high school. Adonis was one of the top lawyers New York had to offer and had gotten Klax out of more trouble than could be counted on *both* hands. Once a small, scrawny kid with glasses, Adonis had grown into what most women called "fine as hell." He was tall with brown skin, and the dimples that came along with his smile made the girls go wild. Adonis was the type that preferred not to get his hands dirty, but he would if he had to. Still, Klax tried not to involve Adonis in any of his dealings unless necessary.

"I see Jessica must have let you out of the house," Klax shot back. "What time you gotta be home, midnight?"

"Oooh! I see you got jokes!" Adonis laughed and slapped hands with Klax.

"You know I'm just fuckin' with you, G. I like Jessica, even though I always thought you would marry a brown queen with a phat-ass booty," Klax said making a pear shape in the air with his hands.

"We're not married yet," Adonis said, eyeing a chocolate woman shaking her rear with her friends. "What Jessica doesn't know won't hurt her."

"Whatever happened to marrying for love and not riches?"

"That went out the window when a millionaire fell in love with me," Adonis answered with a grin. "Now, congrats on your new club, my brother, but if you'll excuse me, I think that fine black thing right there needs some attention."

He tried to make his way down from the VIP section, but Dame stopped him by putting a hand on his chest.

"Not tonight, boss," Dame said and made it so that Adonis couldn't get past him.

"What you mean not tonight?" Adonis asked, turning his face up like Russell Westbrook. "I'm a grown-ass man."

He tried to get past Dame again, but that time, Klax caught him by the arm. When Adonis looked at him, Klax nodded to the dance floor. To the untrained eye, Klax's soldiers moving through the cluster of people would have been camouflaged, but not to Adonis's. He had been around Klax too long not to know when a move was being made. He raised his brow and shot Klax a confused look.

"Like he said, not tonight, boss," Klax said and grabbed a bottle of champagne off of the circular glass table behind him.

"What's going on?" Adonis asked as he watched his friend take a swig of the liquid.

"Some unauthorized moves have been being made. And whoever is behind them has been specifically targeting Harlem."

"Do you know who it is?"

"Nah, not—" Dame started, but Klax interrupted him.

"That young nigga in the center of that group over there by the wall. In the white jacket."

The person that Klax was talking about was looking up at them as they stared back down at him. He looked out of place. He was standing with his hands clasped and shoulders back as if he were waiting for someone. No . . . as if he wanted to be seen. If he wanted to make a move to leave, it was too late because Klax's young soldiers had already spotted him. Klax watched as his men approached the young man and grabbed him by his arm. His own goons surrounding him stood up, but quickly realized they were outnumbered when the rest of Klax's soldiers showed up. White Jacket put his arms up and his weapons, as well as the weapons of those who were with him, were stripped. He then nodded his head to the man who had his arm and allowed himself to be escorted away.

"That's surprising," Adonis noted as the men walked toward Klax's VIP section. "He just let himself get grabbed?"

"I was expecting a little rah-rah," Klax said and sat down on a couch. "I thought it was gon' look like the Fourth of July in this bitch."

Adonis too sat down while Dame stood over them like a watchdog. It didn't take long for Klax's soldiers to reach him, and when they did, he waved for White Jacket to come up and join him. Although unarmed, the man stepped forward with his head held high and clasped his hands together in front of him. He was about Klax's height, light skin with hazel eyes. The long hair on his head was twisted in neat locs that hung slightly past his shoulders. His eyes skimmed over Adonis and fell on Klax's.

"What's this about?" he asked, shrugging his shoulders.

"We ask the questions," Dame barked and pointed at the seat across from Klax. "Take some of that base out ya voice and sit down."

When he didn't budge, Dame touched his waist and flashed the butt of his gun.

"If you don't wanna comply, we can take you to the basement with the rest of the people you came with. Or should I say, with their corpses. I doubt they're still breathing."

That seemed to get White Jacket's attention. His jaw clenched tightly, and he shot Dame a scornful look, but he finally obliged to the command. He sat in the leather chair and averted his attention back to Klax.

"Are you who I think you are?" Klax asked.

"I don't know what you're talking about, boss." White Jacket put his hands in the air. "Maybe this is a case of mistaken identity. If I wasn't who you assumed, and your people just killed half a dozen innocent men, how would *you* feel?"

"Just bodies in the cross fire," Klax shrugged. "But I don't think they were innocent. Nah . . . not by how bright you are. Came in here looking like Snow Patrol and shit. Now, answer me. Are you the one who's been hitting my spots?"

"If I am?"

"I would say you are one bold mothafucka stepping in my spot tonight."

"I guess you can call me one bold mothafucka then," White Jacket said with a smile. "Yeah, I'm the one who ordered those hits."

"What, your mother never told you that you can't go around claiming what isn't yours?"

"Nah, she didn't get the chance to. But I guess your father missed that lesson too."

"What's your name? Before I kill you, I'd like to know your identity."

"I'll give you my name, but not because you'll get the chance to kill me, but because I want you and all of Harlem to know my name. My name is LaTron Walker; Tron for short. And I'm here to take back what's rightfully mine."

"And that would be?" Klax asked, unable to hide the fact that he was slightly tickled.

"Harlem," Tron said simply. "The same Harlem your father stole from mine twenty-three years ago."

"My dad ain't steal shit, and if he did, oh well. You snooze, you lose," Klax said, rubbing his hands together.

"You snooze you lose? Is that right?"

"That's right."

"Sounds like some shit the son of a pussy-ass nigga would say."

"I'm gon' ignore that disrespect to my pops. What I'm more concerned with is how I'ma make you pay for all the damage you've caused throughout my city. I'm thinking a bullet through the temple. Short and clean. You'll die instantly, so you probably won't feel any pain. I think that's fair, don't you?"

"I thought you'd be so arrogant," Tron laughed. "I figured that you wouldn't take me seriously, but you should. That throne you're sitting on? You're only keeping it warm for me. And another thing . . . I'm leaving here the same way I came in." He casually made a motion with his hand and smiled.

"Boss," Dame said in a shocked voice. "Look."

He pointed at Klax's chest, and when Klax looked down, he saw a small red dot moving slowly up his chest and to his face. He glanced around and saw that it wasn't only him who had a beam on him. Both Adonis and Dame did too. Klax felt his chest tighten with a rage that he'd never felt before.

"Fire on me, and you'll be dead before I hit the ground," Klax growled.

"I know," Tron grinned. "Don't worry, King; this is just insurance that I'ma make it out of here tonight. The war starts soon. Nice chat."

With that, he grabbed the bottle of liquor from the glass table that separated him from Klax and stood up. He walked toward the man guarding the VIP exit, and Klax angrily nodded his head for his soldier to let Tron out.

"Oh, and tell your people to let my niggas go. I saw what you did to my youngin yesterday. I didn't like that. Nice club, by the way," Tron threw over his shoulder.

"I'll be seeing you," Klax said loud enough for him to hear. "And next time, ain't no crimson trace gon' stop me from knocking your head from your shoulders."

Chapter 4

"Because an illusion is an illusion, reality always exists despite the façade."

—Kanye West

Tron

Tron walked out of the club, feeling like a million bucks. His men had orders not to release their aim on Klax Turner until he was safely out of the building. Klax had done a good job on security . . . on the ground, anyway. Tron knew it would be hard for his people to pose as security where Klax could see them. If he were as sharp as Tron thought, he'd be able to out an imposter in a quickness. However, the security on the second floor of the club was easy to lure away from their posts. All it took was a couple of hundred dollars to have two beautiful women to get them to follow them into a supply closet. Once there, the men were met with a deadly surprise. Klax would hopefully find their bodies before they started stinking. Tron's men then stole their Diamond Club vests and resumed their posts, waiting for their signal.

As he requested, the rest of his men were released and left the club with him. None of their weapons were given back to them, but that was all right. There were plenty more where they came from. They all filed out behind him, and Tron knew the smartest thing would be for them all to shake the spot.

"Fan out," he told them, and they dispersed.

There was a long line of people standing outside waiting to get in the club, and he noticed the hungry eyes of many women on him. He ignored their gazes and catcalls as he walked toward the valet. A young man who didn't even look old enough to get inside Diamonds took his ticket for Tron's 2018 black Ferrari 488 GTB. As he waited for his vehicle, something caught his eye. Well, more like someone. A woman. It caught him by surprise because his eyes normally weren't swayed easily by beauty. But she might have been the most dazzling thing he'd ever seen. She was bad, so bad that he had to step in front of her as she walked by him. He'd never wanted to be an article of clothes in his life, but the way her jeans hugged her curves had him envious. She was in the middle of cutting the line with her friend to walk inside the club but stopped because he was in her way.

"Excuse me," she said and tried to go around him, but he stepped in front of her. "Excuse *you.*"

"I'm sorry, I just had to get one last look at you before you walked right past me," Tron said, taking her hand and kissing her knuckles. "I mean no disrespect. Have fun tonight, beautiful."

"You one of them weird niggas or something?" she said.

"Never weird, shorty," Tron chuckled. "Just mesmerized. You have the kind of beauty that could make the world stop."

"Uh-huh," she said and eyed him curiously. "Well, if I'm so beautiful, aren't you gonna ask for my name?"

"One day," he said with a smile.

He let her hand go and stepped out of her way so she could pass. By that time, his car had pulled up, and he could feel the woman's eyes on him as he walked to the driver's side.

"Uh-uh. Do not let that nigga's weak-ass game get you," he heard her homegirl say behind him. "Let's get up in here and dance our asses off. Wait, that's his 'Rari?"

He chuckled to himself when his car pulled up. Women were all the same. It didn't take much to impress them. A nice outfit, a nice car . . . It was all the same. As long as it looked like you had money, it didn't matter to them. When he glanced back, he gave the woman he had spoken to a knowing look and instantly, her full lips formed into a line.

"My brother had that car when he was 16; boss up," she said loudly and turned toward the club.

Tron watched the way her thighs jiggled as she walked away from him and found himself still smiling. Maybe she wasn't that easy, after all.

"The princess strikes again," the valet said and handed him his car keys.

"What?" Tron asked, confused.

"You don't know who you were just talking to, man? That's Kleigh Turner's fine ass. She's the princess of Harlem."

"Turner? As in Klax Turner?"

"Yup. That's his baby sister. I don't know one nigga that's been able to get at her."

"You don't say," Tron said, rubbing his chin as he watched her disappear into the club. "Maybe I'll try my luck."

"Yeah, right. Klax is the big bad wolf around here."

"Even the big bad wolf had his day," Tron said and got in his car without another word.

He had planned to tear down Klax's operation from the outside, but now he had a better idea. Twenty-three years ago when Kameron Turner ordered the hit on the infamous Sunny Walker, he didn't know he had created an even bigger monster. When Tron's father took a bullet to the head for his son all those years back, he was left for dead . . . but he didn't die. After the attack, he was left with a silver plate in his head and had to relearn to do basic motor functions. When he was back and well enough to get back in the game, he didn't. It had cost him too much. Seeing his wife and daughter murdered in front of him had changed him. He didn't want anything to do with the drug game anymore, and more so, he didn't want his son to follow in his footsteps. But some wishes were just too grand to grant. Tron was everything Sunny had been in his prime, but better. He had the swagger of a boss and the fearless heart to match. Once Tron found out what a legend his old man had been, he vowed to avenge him for everything they'd both lost.

Sunny had moved them from Harlem to Albany when Tron was 8 years old. They lived a good life with the money Sunny had in the bank. Sunny started a local training gym for boxers. It was meant to be a place where troubled youth could go to evade the streets. The same streets he couldn't save his son from. To Tron, "good" could have always been "better." No, it *should* have been better. When Sunny refused to teach him everything he knew about the game, Tron took it upon himself to learn it hands-on when he was 18. With the help of his uncle Kyan, Tron rose up in ranks until he felt that he was ready to go at Kameron Turner . . . only to find out that Kameron had died and left his empire to his son, Klax. Tron lived most of his life knowing that he was the true heir of Harlem, and that knowledge alone doused the flame burning inside of him.

As he drove, his thoughts fell to Kleigh Turner. His interest in her had piqued, but not just because she was beautiful. She was a key, and that meant she was more valuable than gold or diamonds to him. There was no way he was going to let his link to the throne slip from between his fingers. He wasn't going to tear Klax's empire down from the outside. He was going to do it from within.

He was staying in an apartment in Manhattan since it was close to his mark. He always figured plain sight was the best hiding spot, not to mention that it was a complex owned by his father with a gated parking garage. When Tron got there, he showed the man in charge of manning the gate his parking permit. Tron had gotten to know him as Timothy. He was a stout, dark-skinned man with a thick mustache that had many gray hairs entangled in it. The top of his head was completely bald, and the moonlight gleamed off the top of it.

"Late night, Mr. Walker?" Timothy said, handing the permit back to Tron.

Tron checked his watch and saw that it was just then about to be two in the morning. He smiled to himself knowing that Klax probably had people scouring New York trying to find him. He shrugged his shoulders and placed the small plastic card back in his wallet.

"Young niggas gotta have fun too."

"I know that's right, youngblood," Timothy said with a grin. "Just don't hurt 'em too bad. With a car like this here, you're bound to catch a hater or two."

"Word," Tron said. Timothy let the gate up. "You good out here? You need me to order you some food or something?"

"Nah, man, I'm good. My wife sends me to work fucked and fed every night," Timothy answered, and both men laughed.

"Sounds like you have a keeper. I'll get at you another time."

With that, he rolled his window back up, drove through the gate, and down the ramp to the brightly lit up parking garage. He parked in the spot that had his last name painted on the yellow cement stopper. His parking spot was convenient because it was right next to the elevator that took him right to the floor of his apartment. He got out and locked his car doors, heading for the elevator. After the night he'd had, the only thing on his mind right then was his soft king bed and silk sheets. He knew the grounds like the back of his hand since it was where he lived with his father for two years before they moved. Sunny not only bought the complex, but he had it fixed up and turned into a luxurious property. Tron had been young, but he remembered what a drastic change it had been moving from their large home in Harlem to the apartment. Without his mother and sister, the place always felt empty. He couldn't count the number of times he woke up in a sweat from the nightmares of their murders. Those were the saddest two years of his life. The only thing he learned was how to keep his feelings bottled up. His performance in school noticeably plummeted, and his social interactions were nonexistent. He didn't want to let anyone close to him ever again. The pain of his loss was too much for a young boy to handle.

When Sunny saw that Tron wasn't getting any better, he moved them to Albany. After they settled in their new dwellings, Tron knew his father to seldom return to the complex. Tron always wondered if Sunny feared that Kameron would come back to finish the job he started, but he never asked. Sunny hired someone to oversee the property and even to do the hiring process for the employees working in the leasing office. Despite being part owner of the place, Tron found comfort in the fact that nobody there knew his face. Although his last name too was Walker, nobody seemed to make the connection that he was Arnold Walker's son. He was ideally able to move in and out without question.

He took the elevator up to the third floor, and when he stepped out, the scent of clean linen hit his nostrils. The light shining from the square light fixtures bounced off of the gray walls, and Tron made a mental note to see about changing the white floor tile to marble. His apartment was at the very end of the hallway, and as he passed each door, he heard the same thing coming from them: nothing. Being that it was so late at night, he was positive that everyone was either sleeping or not there at all.

Tron reached his apartment, but upon applying pressure to put the key in the hole, instead, the door pushed open. It caught him by surprise, and he became still, listening for any movement on the inside, but he heard nothing. However, the hairs on the back of his neck instantly stood up and let him know that *somebody* was inside. He grabbed the tool from his waist and slowly pushed the door all the way open. His bedroom light was on, and he knew for a fact that he'd turned it off before he left. He crept inside and shut the door quietly behind him. Whoever had made the mistake of breaking into his home wouldn't get a chance to correct it because Tron wasn't letting them leave alive. He cocked his pistol as he stealthily walked toward the bedroom and raised it when he came up on the closed door. Just as he was about to kick it open, he heard quick footsteps come up behind him. He tried to turn around and see who it was, but a quick jab to his right shoulder prevented that. The blow was a powerful one and made him drop his gun. He tried to turn around again but stopped when he felt a gun against the back of his locs. He let what would probably be his last breath out of his mouth, knowing that one of Klax's soldiers must have found him. But then, he heard a voice that changed everything.

"You're off your game. Any other nigga woulda blew your brains out."

The deep voice was a familiar one. So familiar that a smirk formed on Tron's face. When he felt the pressure of the gun leave his head, he turned around and faced the man that helped raise him.

"Uncle Kyan," he said, and the older man pulled him in for an embrace. "It's like two in the morning. What are you doing here?"

"I could ask you the same thing. Ya old man thinks you're down in Denver for some boxing tournament. I knew that was a lie."

"And how did you come to that conclusion?" Tron said, picking up his gun and going back into the living room.

"Because you've always been the type to like being *in* the fight, not *watching* it."

"Yeah, yeah. You always did think you knew me better than my own pops," Tron said and turned on a tall lamp before sitting down. He placed his gun on the glass coffee table and motioned toward the red love seat across from him. "You can go on 'head and take a seat."

"Don't mind if I do," Kyan said, tucking his gun in his waist before sitting down on the love seat.

"If you knew I wouldn't be in Denver, how *did* you know where to find me?" Tron asked when his uncle was situated.

Kyan leaned back in his seat and observed his nephew. Black didn't crack, because although he was in his mid-forties, he still had a youthful look about him. The hair on his head was still jet black, although Tron often presumed that he got it dyed. Still, his waves and crisp line put many young hustlers to shame. That night, he wore a slim, olive-green tailored suit with a white button-up and gray tie. On his feet were studded Rollerboy Christian Louboutins, gray to match his tie. He placed his right ankle on top of his left knee and gave Tron an amused look.

"It was easy."

"How?"

"You do know I help ya old man with this place? He owns it; I run it. So, imagine my shock when my nephew's credit report ran across my desk. I thought to myself, 'Now, why on earth would Tron be tryna get an apartment when he's owned a house since he was 20?' And then, since you know ya uncle's ear is always to the streets, I started hearing about some niggas wreaking havoc on Harlem's kingpin. And I just put two and two together from there."

"Does Pop know?" Tron asked.

He could have shot himself in the foot for being so stupid as far as the apartment went. His father wouldn't go for it if he knew what Tron was really doing. He couldn't even say what Sunny would do in his rage if he found out, so Tron hoped he didn't know already.

"Should he?"

"Nah."

"Give me one good reason why he shouldn't know. If you can do that, I'll rethink telling him who his new tenant is," Kyan said and clasped his hands together.

"How do I know you aren't just tryna figure out my moves so you can tell him anyway?"

"You should know both of us better than that, neph. Plus, if Sunny knew you had lied to him in the first place, it would be him on this couch and not me. But keep in mind, he's only one call away."

"A'ight," Tron sighed and shook his head. "A'ight, man. I'll tell you."

He paused, and Kyan cleared his throat.

"I'm waiting," he said and looked at his gold watch for emphasis.

"I came here to settle an old score."

"An old score?" Kyan raised an eyebrow.

"Yeah, you heard right. I'm here to take Harlem back. Like you and me used to talk about."

On Tron's last sentence, Kyan burst out laughing so hard that he had to hold his stomach. He tried to speak a few times but exploded into more fits of laughter. When he was finally done, he wiped the tears from his eyes and looked into Tron's hard face.

"Oh shit. You're serious about this, neph?"

"I wouldn't be here if I weren't."

"That's *suicide,* youngin," Kyan told him. "These streets—"

"What about these streets? They ain't no joke? Well, news flash, Unc, I ain't neither. You know that. You know me."

"Still," Kyan said, "tryna take back Harlem?"

"What do you think I've been doin' the past five years? Moving up in the ranks for nothing? That little operation back in Albany ain't got shit on what we can do here. The market here is unlimited; I'm capped there. Plus, as I said, it's time to take back what's mine."

"Yours?"

"Yeah. *Mine.* Kameron Turner took everything from my father, set his son in my seat, and gave his daughter the life that was stolen from my sister. I'ma kill Klax Turner, and have New York's connect come through me to distribute work."

"A'ight," Kyan said as if something was wracking his brain.

"A'ight?"

"I won't tell Sunny. If he knew this is what you were doing, a hell would rise in New York that isn't even in the Bible."

"Thanks, Unc."

"I'm not finished," Kyan said, rubbing his chin. "I won't tell Sunny *for now,* but this secret has a limited hold time with me. If this is what you're tryna do, hitting a few stash spots and trap houses ain't gon' cut it. That ain't gon' do nothing but make the dragon mad and call in reinforcements. Nah, if you're gon' do it, you gotta do it swift and right. You gotta kill Kevin Klax Turner before he kills you."

"I know," Tron said, wrapping his head around the thought.

The only reason he didn't kill Klax in the club that night was that he too would have met an untimely death. He almost told Kyan about what had just taken place but thought better of it. He wouldn't have thought too kindly about Tron being unarmed and in danger, even though he had it under control.

"I'll use some of the connects I have around town to try to get any information that might assist you."

"Thanks, Unc. You know something?"

"What's up?"

"I never understood why my dad walked away from it all. I know this ain't the life he wants for me. He wanted me to be some kind of Ivy League nigga, wearing suspenders and shit. That ain't me. I remember sitting up with y'all late at night, counting endless stacks of money. The family trips we would go on, it all just seemed so limitless. I don't know who in their right mind would give all that up."

"I'll tell you who would . . . Someone who lost it all. Sunny watched them gun your mama and sister down right there in front of him. Watching your mama bleed out and die was some shit that changed me forever. So I can only imagine what losing her did to him. That's why he never even wanted you to touch the drug game. He knows how addictive it is. He was an addict, and it cost him much more than he was willing to pay."

"And that's why he can't know about what I'm doing here until I do it. I don't want him to try to stop me. He had his reasons for giving up what was his, and I have mine for fighting for it. This ain't just about him. It's about the mother I never had and the sister who still visits me in my dreams. How much time can you buy me?"

"As much as I can. And if instead of having a crown on your head at the end of this, you end up dead or in jail, just call me Bennet."

"Bennet?"

"Yeah, nigga, 'cause I ain't in it. Sunny ain't about to have my head on a chopping block because his dumb-ass son wants some notoriety. This is where I leave you." Kyan stood up and went to the front door. When he opened it, he turned around before he left. "You got two weeks, you hear me?"

"Loud and clear."

Chapter 5

"Every new beginning comes from some other beginning's end."

—Anonymous

Kleigh

She couldn't get his voice out of her head. She could almost feel the vibrations from its deep baritone on her skin as she lay in her bed alone. After the club, Bahli had gone home, and Kleigh did the same. The two had been having a good time shaking what their mothers gave them, but their night was cut short when Klax saw them. She couldn't believe that out of all the clubs, Bahli had directed her to Klax's.

"How was I supposed to know the newest spot in the city belonged to your brother when *you* didn't?"

Which was true. Klax had his hands in so many businesses that Kleigh couldn't keep up sometimes. Once he spotted them inside Diamonds, not only did he make them leave, but he now knew about Kleigh's new car and how she'd been able to sneak out. It was just another moment of how annoying it was to be his little sister, and although she did as she was told and left, she knew it wouldn't be the last time she heard about it. However, Klax and his God complex were far from her mind. All she could think about was the man with the peanut butter skin and locs. He hadn't even asked for her name. She didn't know why that bothered her so much. Maybe because most men wouldn't even approach her, but he did. So why limit himself? She tried to push the memory of that night to the furthest corner of her mind and rolled over, drifting off to sleep.

She felt like she'd only been asleep ten minutes when she heard the front door to her home slam shut. When she blinked her sleepy eyes open, she was shocked to see the rays of sunlight peeping through the wooden blinds on her window. Kleigh groaned to herself when she grabbed her phone and saw that the time read ten in the morning. Not only had she overslept, she still felt like she needed at least five more hours of shut-eye. She noticed that she had five missed calls from her brother and a few from Bahli, but still, she didn't have to guess who had burst in her home.

"All that sneaking around got you tired, huh?"

Kleigh pulled the covers back over her head at the sound of Klax's voice. She groaned even louder that time and wished that he would go away. When she peeked at the doorway to her room, she saw him standing there with his arms crossed, and she rolled her eyes.

"I just woke up. Can we do this another time?" she pleaded with him. "You act like it's a crime for me to want to go out."

"It is when it's a nigga moving against me right now," Klax said and snatched the covers from off of her. "So, nah, we gon' do this right now."

"Stop! And how am I supposed to know that?"

The T-shirt and pair of shorts she had on did nothing to keep her warm, and her attitude hit her almost as fast as the cold air did. She sat up and pushed her hair out of her face so that she could glare at him.

"Don't look at me like that," Klax warned.

"I'll do what I want. Oh wait, I can't because I have to stop my life because you don't have your shit on lock!"

"Watch your mouth," he told her. "Until this problem is taken care of, I need to know where you are at all times. That's not up for debate."

Kleigh smacked her lips.

"Even after you handle whoever has been hitting your spots, I still won't be able to do shit without running it by my big brother. I don't want to live like this. Do you know how embarrassing it was to have to leave the club last night after not even an hour?"

"You wouldn't have had to leave if you hadn't come to my spot in the first place," he said like it was simple. "Be happy I was busy talking to Adonis because if I would have seen you and Bahli, y'all wouldn't have even got in."

"You're annoying. And when did you even *get* a club?" Kleigh said, jerking her head at him. "It's crazy that you want me to run all of my moves by you, but you don't tell me anything at all."

"Those are the joys of being the king," Klax said with a grin. "And since the king is also your big brother, you won't ever hear me apologizing for going to extra lengths to protect my baby sister—especially with the streets going as crazy as they have been. There won't ever be a time that you look out your window, and you don't see one of my people sitting there. Dad asked me to protect you, and I'm gon' do that until there is no more breath in me, do you understand?"

Kleigh rolled her eyes and got up to head to the kitchen, but Klax caught her by the arm.

"I said, do you understand?"

"Yeah, nigga, damn," she said and snatched her arm away. "But if you grab me like that again, I'm calling Mama. And I don't see why you were so mad about me being in the club last night anyway. I mean, if it's *your* club, that should be one of the safest places for me."

She walked past him and went into the kitchen to find something to feed her growling stomach. She'd only had a few shots of Patrón the night before, but it was on an empty stomach. From her refrigerator, she pulled out a carton of eggs and a pack of bacon.

"Since you're here, without invitation, might I add, you might as well have breakfast with me," she said when Klax sat at her glass dining room table. "Pancakes or toast?"

"Toast," he answered. "And leave a little fat on my bacon."

"You got it, King," Kleigh said sarcastically and got busy over the stove.

As she cooked, she kept sneaking glances at her brother. As usual, he was clean from head to toe in his usual designer outfit, but something was off about him. He wasn't the type to wear a continuous frown on his face, nor was he the type to seem worried, and he was doing both right then. When she finished cooking, she made their plates, then set them down on the table and went to pour two tall glasses of orange juice.

"Here," she said and handed him his glass.

"Thanks, baby sis," he said and took a long gulp.

She sat down in the seat to the right of him and took a sip from her glass. The siblings ate in silence before it became deafening to Kleigh. She cleared her throat and looked at her brother. He paid her no mind, and it was almost as if he hadn't even heard her. So she cleared her throat again. That time, she tapped his hand gently.

"Earth to Klax," she said and waved her fork in his face. "You good?"

"Yeah, I'm straight."

"Lie again," she warned. "What's going on with you? You're acting strange."

"A few hits were ordered on the Bronx and Harlem recently."

"Harlem?" Kleigh asked alarmed. "Who would be crazy enough to do some shit like that? Did they get anything?"

"Nah," Klax answered, and Kleigh knew she probably wasn't going to get any more out of him.

"Be easy. You know you're going to catch the person responsible. Whoever he is, he's gonna slip up eventually."

"He already did," Klax said, and suddenly, he stopped eating. He gripped the fork so tightly in his hand that Kleigh was sure that she saw it bend. "He showed up at the club last night. He said . . ."

"What?" Kleigh asked and leaned toward him. "What did he say, Klax?"

Klax blinked and looked up as if he abruptly had remembered where he was. He took one more bite of his eggs and stood up from the table. Leaning down, he kissed her lovingly on the forehead.

"Don't worry about it. I have it handled," he assured her. "Enough about me. How's business at the bakery?"

"Booming," Kleigh said proudly. "The mayor just placed a huge catering order for her fortieth birthday."

"I guess all Mama's recipes were some good after all then, huh?"

"Hey, hey!" Kleigh raised an eyebrow at him. "Don't give her all the credit. Some of the recipes are mine too."

"Whatever you say. Speaking of the bakery, why aren't you there?"

"Jasmine has been opening on Fridays," Kleigh said speaking of her store manager. "I come in a little later in the afternoon. I *did* want to go in a little early today, though, but I overslept. But, you know, when you're the boss, you can do shit like that."

"I feel it. Anyways, thanks for breakfast. I need to go handle some business."

"Whatever," Kleigh said, rolling her eyes at him.

"Keep playing, and those things are gon' get stuck like that one day," Klax told her walking to the door.

"Klax! Wait," she said before he was gone. "Dude coming to the club, is that why you wanted me to leave? Did you think he was gon' do something to me?"

"Ain't nobody ever gon' touch you. Believe that," Klax said in all seriousness. He stepped out of the condo and waved a hand before the door shut all the way. "Love you!"

"Yeah yeah yeah," Kleigh huffed and dropped the fork on the plate in front of her. "You love me enough to leave me with your dishes."

She should have known he wasn't going to tell her everything that was happening in his line of business. Kleigh wondered if he knew that by keeping her in the loop would be way less stressful for him. Even though she was grown, he still viewed her as his kid sister. She loved how her brother loved her, but sometimes she thought he forgot that he wasn't her father. Still, she would respect his wishes until the noise in the streets died down. The last thing she wanted was to be taken hostage by some maniac who had a vendetta against her brother.

Kleigh cleared the table and commenced to getting dressed for the day. When she was back in her bedroom, before she got in the shower, she grabbed her phone from the unmade bed. She figured she'd better call Bahli back before she pulled a Klax Turner and pulled up on her unexpectedly. The phone rang only twice before her friend answered.

"Bitch, I should have been childish and sent you to voicemail," Bahli's terse voice said. "I know you saw me calling you!"

"I just got up not too long ago. Damn, a bitch can't even get no sleep?"

"No! Especially after your brother ruined our night. You had me get dressed to dance for about thirty minutes."

"My bad," Kleigh said, feeling genuinely sorry. "But going to Diamonds was *your* idea. But at least we know for next time."

"Uh-huh. I guess I'll forgive you. But only because barely anybody saw me in that dress, which means I can wear it again!"

"You know what? You are a mess, okay?" Kleigh said with a giggle.

"I'm just being real, girl. Why was Klax tripping so hard anyway? You would think that since it was his club, he'd feel more comfortable that you were there and not at another spot, you know?"

"That's exactly what I said when he stopped by this morning. I guess yelling at me in the middle of the club wasn't enough. He had to come to finish his point."

"That brother of yours is a trip. He acts like he's your dad or something."

"Yeah . . ." Kleigh's voice trailed off, and she thought about what Klax had said. "Apparently, some dude who've been tryna get at him was in the club last night."

"Oh, word? It's like that? What was he doing there?"

"I don't know," Kleigh answered as she pulled a matching bra and underwear set from her drawer. "You know my brother doesn't tell me shit. Whatever is going on, Klax ain't at ease about it. I've never seen my brother look so old in the face."

"Well, whoever dude is, I hope he's ready to be in a world of hurt. We all know Klax doesn't play that shit. What did he say about your car?"

"Nothing at all, shockingly."

"Probably because he already put a tracker on it," Bahli laughed loudly.

"You know what? I'm about to hang up this phone."

"Whaaat? You know your crazy-ass brother is good for it," Bahli said still giggling. "Bitch, you gon' be tryna get some dick, and Klax is gon' pull up like, sike! You thought!"

"Well, we both know that's not going to happen anytime soon," Kleigh said, entering the bathroom in her bedroom and sitting down on the toilet.

"I wouldn't be so sure. You saw the way that guy was staring at you last night. The one we saw right before we went into the club."

"I know who you're talking about," Kleigh told her.

"His approach was kind of weird, but I think he was really mesmerized by you," Bahli said in a dreamy tone. "What that nigga say? Something like, 'I just had to stop and get a better look at you.'"

"He actually said, 'I just had to get one last look at you before you walked right past me.'"

"See! Now, *that* was cute."

"Cute? Just last night you were talking about it was some weak-ass game."

"Girl, you know I was just tryna hurry up and get in the club! You should have still gave him your number. Driving a car like that, baby boy is sitting on some mean paper."

"Bahli, I don't need a nigga for his money."

"You don't need a broke boy either. A paid bitch needs a paid nigga. Period!"

"True that."

"Bahli! Would you please come show me how to work the fax machine," Kleigh heard someone in Bahli's background call, and she heard her friend groan loudly.

"Well, baby, duty calls. I'll give you a call later on today. We can get dinner or something."

"Sounds good. Love you."

"Love you too."

Kleigh disconnected the phone and set it down on the long counter to the sink. She put her hair in two tight cornrows before getting in the shower and placed a black cap over them. After that, she stripped down and got in the shower. As the steaming hot water hit and slid down her body, once again, her eyes went to the guy from the night before. She didn't know why she wished she'd gotten his name. Normally, she forgot about the guys that tried to holler at her. None of them had left a lasting impression. But he, the person who had only said one sentence to her, had. Maybe it was the fact that he didn't try to press up on her. What if he was genuinely just complimenting her, and that was it? Maybe he had a wife at home, and that's why he didn't press Kleigh for her contact information. That was the only viable reason she could think of for any man not shooting a real shot with her. Kleigh shook her narcissistic thoughts to the side. It *was* possible for a man to be a gentleman; however, she had just never experienced anything like it before.

She finished washing up and got out of the shower to get dressed. She dried her body off with one of the soft towels her mother had gotten for her when she first moved in and the moisturized her body with coconut oil. She almost laughed at herself when the steam cleared on the mirror, and she saw herself in her underwear and cap on her head.

"I look a mess," she said and picked up her toothbrush.

As she brushed her teeth, she left the bathroom for a moment and went to her closet. There, she grabbed the long Malaysian lace wig she planned on wearing for the day. It was jet black and silky smooth to the touch with a middle part. She'd named it Megan and took care of it the way she did her natural hair. She went back to the bathroom to spit and brush her straight white teeth. Once she finished, she placed the toothbrush back in its holder and put the wig on her head. She used clips to install it rather than glue because she valued her edges.

Once Kleigh was confident that it was securely in place, she smoothed out the baby hairs to give a more natural finish. When she was done, you couldn't even tell it wasn't her hair.

It took Kleigh twenty more minutes to leave the house since she got distracted taking selfies in her full-length mirror. But when she did, she looked as if she had just stepped off a runway. At the bakery, she required her employees to dress in standard work attire, which included a pair of tan slacks and shirt with the company logo and name, Turner's Bakery. She, on the other hand, wore whatever she wanted. That day, she'd opted for a pair of dark blue jeans that made her hips and bottom pop, with a thin strap black body suit and a black leather jacket. A pair of pointed-toe black Louboutin heels were on her feet, and the red Gucci cross body purse matched the bottom of her shoes and her lipstick. Her hair went down to her backside and swished back and forth as she walked.

"Hello, Miss Turner," Donald, the doorman said when he saw her step off the elevator. "Off to the bakery?"

Donald was a Caucasian man in his fifties with a head full of gray hair. He'd been working as the doorman to the condo since years before Kleigh had even moved in. He wasn't a bad-looking man, and he always seemed to be in a pleasant mood whenever Kleigh saw him.

"Yes, I am!" Kleigh said as she walked past him and out of the glass swivel doors. "I'll try to bring you back a cake. I'm trying a new recipe out."

"You know I don't mind being a guinea pig," he said and patted his slightly pudgy belly. "Beggars can't be choosers. Have a nice day!"

Kleigh waved to him and walked to one of two of her parking spots. The pink BMW M5 Klax bought for her seemed to be waiting for her. She loved that car. Not only was pink her favorite color, but the all-black interior really set the ride off. It was a real-life Barbie car, and she loved pushing it in traffic. When she got in, she paired her phone with the car, turned on some music, and pulled out of the parking garage. She found herself lost in the melodic voice of Summer Walker the entire drive to the bakery in Harlem.

"I just need some dick. I just need some love. Tired of fucking with these lame niggas, baby. I just need a thug."

Kleigh was still singing along with the artist when she pulled into the alley in the back of the building. She got out of the car and entered the bakery through the back door. Turner's Bakery wasn't a huge establishment, more like comfy. On the inside was the kitchen, of course, in the back, the hot-and-ready section, the cashier's counter, and in the front were a few tables for customers to eat at. The aroma of goodies baking hit her nostrils, and she savored it the way she always did, like it was her first time. She walked through the kitchen and headed toward her office in the very back.

"Hey, boss!" Eddy, her godfather, and her best baker, shouted.

Kleigh gave the older man a big smile and waved at him. He was one of her mother's oldest friends and one of the reasons Kleigh loved baking so much. He was also her dad's first cousin and the one who had gotten her parents together in the first place. Eddy stood at about five foot seven and wore his curly hair cut short. His smooth, toffee-colored skin was flawless, and he was so pretty and always so well-groomed that when Kleigh was growing up, she would ask him for beauty tips and not her mother. He stood there in his work attire, white apron and white baker's hat, looking like he was just made for the job. Growing up, he said since everyone always told him he had sugar in his tank, why not load that same sugar into the sweets that everyone loved so much. Little did Klax know, most of the recipes their mother used were Eddy's.

"Eddy, today is your off day. What are you doing here?" she asked, going to him and hugging him.

"I couldn't leave y'all high and dry with the mayor's big order tomorrow," he told her and motioned to his cluttered workstation. "It's been crazy back here in this kitchen, and I figured while the other bakers are placing regular customer orders, I could get a head start on the big Kahuna."

"Thank you! That's why I love you so much, even though we both know you just want to take credit for the red velvet cake," she said with a wink.

"Girl, you know can't nobody make that cake like me! The mayor's eyes are going to roll to the back of her head after one bite, I assure you of that!" he said, placing his hand on his hip and playfully rolling his neck.

"Uh-huh," Kleigh said with a giggle. "Uncle Charlie must have put you in a good mood this morning."

"He always does," Eddy said speaking fondly of his husband. "Speaking of which, he wants you, your mom, and your brother to come to the house sometime soon. It's been awhile since we all had dinner. I don't know why your mama is acting like we aren't forever family."

"She took Daddy's death really hard," Kleigh said, unable to hide the brief sadness in her voice. "I mean, we all did, but she lost the love of her life. I don't know if you ever get over that."

"You don't. But staying cooped in the house doesn't help either. It's been two years. It's time for her to breathe some fresh air again. Can't change the past; only can live for a better future."

"I'll tell her you said that, wise guy," Kleigh said to him and kissed him on the cheek.

"Please do. We really miss y'all. I pray for that hot-headed brother of yours every day. I don't want him to end up like his daddy," Eddy told her and snapped his fingers toward her feet. "But *you*, Miss Thing, are working those heels, honey. I'm so proud of you. If I ever had a daughter, she would be just like you. I love you, honey."

"I love you too," she said. "I'm going to let you get back to doing your thing. I need to go check last week's numbers."

"All right, honey. Oh, and you need to check your girl, Jasmine. She thinks that little title of hers means she can talk to motherfuckas all crazy. I'ma show her crazy the next time she comes at me funny."

"Oh, no!" Kleigh said, laughing at his serious expression. "Don't worry. I'll talk to her because I do not need my godfather going to jail, even though we do have bail money."

"Mmm-hmm," Eddy said, turning back to his cake mixture. "You better."

Kleigh left the kitchen and finished the journey to her office in the back. It wasn't huge, just big enough for a desk, a computer, and all of the files she kept back there. She wasn't shocked to see Jasmine already back there sitting at the computer. An excel spreadsheet was open on its screen, and she had a pen and notebook, jotting things down.

"Well, hello, there," Kleigh greeted her with a smile.

"Hey, girl," Jasmine said, not looking up from what she was doing. "I didn't know what time you were going to be in today, so I wanted to have these numbers from last week ready for you to view when you got here."

"See, this is why I hired you. Always on top of things, especially the money," Kleigh said, taking a seat in the chair on the opposite side of Jasmine. "That is, unless you're scheming your own cut of bread from the top."

"Oh, now I know you're crazy," Jasmine said, not batting an eye at Kleigh's bad joke. "I would never do that to you. I value my life too much to play those kinds of games. There! All done."

She slid Kleigh the notebook with the final number from the previous week's sales. When Kleigh saw it, she was more than impressed. They were up 15 percent from the previous week, and the mayor's order was going to put them at a solid 20.

"Good work. I love what I'm seeing," Kleigh said, nodding her head approvingly. "But you do know we have a computer that would have done all this in like five minutes, right?"

"I like math." Jasmine shrugged her shoulders.

Kleigh had known Jasmine since high school, but the two weren't really close back then. They only knew each other because Jasmine's father, James, was Kameron's accountant. James suffered a stroke a few years before Kameron died, and since Kleigh knew he was the primary source of income for the family, she hired Jasmine on at the bakery. She put her in the kitchen at first, but the girl couldn't bake a cake if her life depended on it. In fact, Kleigh was pretty sure that was when the tit for tat between Jasmine and Eddy started. Kleigh soon found out that Jasmine had her father's business savvy and a knack for numbers. Jasmine was made the manager of Turner's Bakery and the person in charge whenever Kleigh was away. It was one of the best business decisions she'd ever made. Although Jasmine and Eddy constantly butted heads, they were all a family, and that's what families did.

Jasmine was not all brains, either. Her beauty wasn't as "in your face" as Kleigh's, but it was there and made her all the more charming. Her tiny nose paired with her deep dimples gave her sandy-brown eyes more of a pop. She had pretty light brown skin that set the tone for the blond highlights she rocked in her pixie haircut.

"Did Eddy tell you about this morning?" Jasmine asked and rolled her eyes. "That sassy motherfucka always wants to fight, I tell you."

"What happened now?"

"He got mad at me because I told him that one of the customers said their cake was dry."

"Oooh," Kleigh said, forming her mouth into an "O."

"I mean, what was I supposed to do?" Jasmine said, putting her hands in the air. "I told him, and he got to cursing me out and telling me 'You think you're Princess Jasmine, but you're more like Apu!'"

"No, he didn't say that!" Kleigh said and began hollering with laughter.

"He did! I couldn't believe his rude ass. I'm just the messenger. And I was *going* to tell him the customer was tripping. I tasted the cake, and it was delicious to me, but you know what? Fuck him and his cake now."

Kleigh was holding her stomach because she was laughing so hard. Those two were definitely a trip. If she didn't know any better, she would think they were blood related by how much they got on each other's nerves.

"You know what, Jas, just stay out of the kitchen today. You know Eddy's ass is crazy. He doesn't play about his cakes."

"Obviously," Jasmine said in a dry tone.

"Y'all will be OK. I need everyone in good moods if everything is going to go smoothly tomorrow evening. I want to make a good impression on the mayor, not just for my sake, but for my brother's."

"Why for him? Is Klax in trouble or something?" Jasmine asked, trying to mask the concern in her voice.

"No. I thought I told you that he's tryna buy that old theater in the Bronx and turn it into a museum. But the council wants to turn it into an apartment complex."

"He wants to turn it into a museum?" Jasmine asked with a wondrous look on her face. "I never pegged Klax as someone interested in that kind of art."

"There are a lot of things about my brother people don't know," Kleigh said.

"I wouldn't mind finding out about them."

"Ooh, girl! I'm going to pretend I didn't hear that," Kleigh said with a laugh and took another look at the notebook. "I'm going to say it again; I'm loving these numbers. So much that I think I'm going to take a trip to the bank early today. You already did morning count, right?"

"Yup. The bag is in the top drawer," Jasmine said, pointing to the file cabinet against the office wall.

"Perfect!"

Kleigh got up and went to the tall, metal gray cabinet. Sure enough, there was a bag of cash right there waiting to get deposited. Kleigh didn't like more than $5,000 to be in the shop at a time. In the morning and early afternoon, there was always double that for a few hours because the deposit didn't get made until two in the afternoon.

"I'm about to make the run," she told Jasmine. "I may or may not be back."

"The joys of being the boss."

"I was going to get in the kitchen for the event tomorrow, but Eddy ain't gon' do nothing but kick me out."

"You have a point there," Jasmine said with a grin.

Kleigh blew her a kiss in farewell before exiting the office. She was about to leave the way she came in, but suddenly, she began to crave a glazed donut. Turning the opposite way, she started toward the front of the bakery and to the hot-and-ready section.

"Hey, Amy, girl," she called to the young lady behind the cash register when she emerged from the back.

"Hey, boss!" the 19-year-old college student shouted back. "I aced my math test!"

"I told you that you would!" Kleigh said, beaming.

Amy was the only white girl in the establishment, but she was raised in the projects and had just as much heart as the rest of them. She even had some spice to her tone and a little booty to match. She was a petite and pretty redhead with a sprinkle of freckles across her nose. Kleigh liked her because she didn't try to be anybody but herself.

"You did," Amy said, leaning against the counter. "I'm not gonna lie, though. I was scared. This was a test that counted toward my final grade."

"Well, you don't need to worry about that now, do you?" Kleigh said, walking around to the hot-and-ready treats and opening the small glass door. "Here, I have something for you."

After she grabbed the donut that she wanted, Kleigh reached into her purse and pulled out two $100 bills. She held them out for Amy to take, but she hesitated.

"Boss, I—"

"Girl, if you don't take this damn money so I can go!" Kleigh told her. "You're off tomorrow since we're closed to do last-minute things with the mayor's event. Go have some fun with your friends on me. And if y'all get a bottle, 'cause you're a college girl, and I know you be drinking. Just be careful."

"Thank you," Amy said and took the money. "I love working here."

"And I love having you here," Kleigh told her, and with one final wave, she was gone.

She decided to leave through the front of the building instead of cutting back through the kitchen. She didn't feel like hearing anymore of Jasmine and Eddy bickering at each other and would rather avoid it at any cost. As soon as she stepped outside, she saw one of Klax's goons parked a little ways away facing the bakery. Sighing, she tucked the metallic gray ziplock bag under her arm as she made her way to the back of the building where her car was parked in the alley. It was a chilly March day, but the beaming sun made it tolerable. Her four-inch heels stabbed the concrete as she walked, making a "clicking" sound as she went down the alley. She saw a few cats run wildly away from behind the bakery's dumpster. The sound of her heels must have startled them since she was the only person there.

Kleigh was almost to her car when a figure jumped from behind the tall dumpster and stood in front of her, blocking her way. She could instantly tell that he was a petty thug, probably from around the way, but still, she was a little nervous since she was alone. She stopped in her tracks and even took a step back to put more distance between them. He wore an all-black hoodie and dirty jeans with a pair of Tims on his feet. It was daytime, but his skin was black as night, and the baby locs on his head stood straight up, making him look like an off-brand Kodak Black.

"Damn, baby, you look and smell like money," he sneered, stepping closer to her. "Why don't you go ahead let me take that bag off ya hands?"

"Nigga, get the fuck out of my way," she said and gestured with her hand for him to move aside. "Some people have shit to do."

She tried to walk around him but stopped when she saw him pull a firearm out from behind his back. She'd seen enough guns to know that the one in his hands was a Mini Draco. Kleigh looked at the gun and then back up at him before turning her lip up.

"Are you dumb? I hope five bands is enough for you to die over. Do you *know* who my brother is?"

"I know exactly who ya big brother is, bitch," he said and spat on the ground next to her feet. "And I don't give a fuck. I'm here to give that nigga grief, starting with you."

Kleigh's nerves suddenly shot to the roof as she remembered Klax saying that somebody was causing him trouble. The thug aimed the gun at her head, making Kleigh duck slightly and put her hands over her head, preparing to hear a gunshot. The split second her eyes were closed, she felt a rush of air as someone came rushing behind her, and the sounds of a tussle began. She opened her eyes to see that someone had come to her rescue—and not just someone. It was the guy from the club the night before.

"You like robbing women, huh?" the newcomer said and hit the thug so hard in his shoulder that he was forced to drop the weapon.

He landed a few more punches before the thug had finally had enough and scurried off down the alley with his blood leaking on the concrete. The guy who saved her bent down and picked up the gun. He examined it for a few moments and chuckled to himself.

"It's not even loaded," his husky voice said. He shook his head. "These young niggas be wilding."

Kleigh stood there and took a few moments to take in what had just happened. Her life had just flashed before her eyes, but there she was . . . still alive and kicking it. She placed a hand over her chest and felt her heart racing. Nothing like that had ever happened to her before, even when she sneaked off from under Klax's watchful eyes. Even though the thug's gun wasn't loaded, she couldn't help but think that he would have found another way to hurt her, and it made her shiver.

"Thank you," she said and checked to make sure she still had all of her belongings. "I don't know where you came from, but I'm glad you showed up."

"No thanks needed," he said, flashing her a dazzling white smile.

"Was this just a right place, right time moment?" she asked.

"I guess you can kind of say that. I actually came by looking for you, and the girl at the register said I'd just missed you, but you parked in the back."

"You came looking for me? How did you even know where to find me?"

"You're a popular girl, Kleigh. Everyone around these parts seems to know who you are. All I had to do was describe your pretty face, and they pointed me to this here bakery."

"Uh-huh," Kleigh said suspiciously.

"Now, I think it may have been fate," he said, and that time when he smiled, Kleigh felt the butterflies in the pit of her stomach flutter.

Had he been that handsome the first time she saw him? No, not handsome. The man was fine. She could tell that he had a fresh line up and retwist in his hair. The light from the sun was hitting the diamonds around his neck just right and made them gleam. He was dressed in a Versace sweatshirt, a pair of jeans, and a pair of black Tims.

"I see you figured out my name, but I still don't know yours," she said.

"That's because I'm a little more low-key than you. I'm Tron."

"Tron?" she asked and made a face.

"Yeah, what's wrong with that?"

"I don't know," she shrugged. "I guess I've never met anybody with that name before."

"And I've never saved a damsel in distress before," Tron teased.

"I was not in that much distress," Kleigh said in denial and walked to the driver door of her car. "But I do appreciate you for showing up when you did. I'm assuming you want some kind of reward now?"

"Nah, not a reward. But I'd say the score would be settled if you let me take you out to dinner tonight."

Kleigh was annoyed with herself by how fast the smile came to her lips. It was so fluent with his question that she couldn't even stop it if she wanted to. He stood back and waited for her answer with the thug's gun in his hands. The slightly smug look on his face told her that he knew her answer before she said it. And she hated that he was right. And she also knew that if her car didn't pull out of the alley soon, the goon Klax had posted outside of the bakery would come looking for her. She sighed and gave in so she could leave.

"All right," she said, pulling her phone out of her purse and handing it to him. "Put your name and number in there, and I'll hit you up if I'm free up. Okay?"

"That's a bet. I'm expecting to hear from you," he said, taking her cell phone for a few moments before giving it back to her. "Now, let me go in here and see what Turner's Bakery is hitting for. If it's trash, I'ma let you know."

"I'm not worried," she said with a wink. "In fact, you might get addicted."

"Is that right?" he asked and licked his lips.

She heard the question but ignored it. Instead, she got in her vehicle and started the engine. When she drove off and glanced in her rearview mirror, she saw him still standing there watching her. The butterflies in her stomach didn't let up until she was on the main street and headed toward the bank. And even then, the smell of his cologne lingered in her nostrils, and his smile flashed in her mind. She grabbed her phone to make sure he really had saved his number there and noticed it was still on the contact screen. When she saw what he saved his number as, she almost swerved the car from laughing so hard.

"Sexy Chunky Peanut Butter," she read out loud. "What the fuck."

She was glad that her windows were tinted because if they weren't, everyone driving next to her would be blinded by her smile. Her teeth were showcased the entire drive to the bank, and in her mind, she knew for sure she wasn't going back to work. She was going to go home and go through her closet to find something to wear that night.

Chapter 6

"Sometimes after a storm, people say there was no warning. There was a warning, but nobody was listening."

—Jeff Last

Tron

It was all staged. The robbery. The rescue. Even him asking her on a date. However, he'd made his young soldier use an unloaded weapon in fear of it going off during the whole altercation. Tron didn't want anything to happen to Kleigh while he was trying to get close to her. When the coast was clear, and he was sure Kleigh was gone, he placed two fingers on his lips and whistled twice. On his call, the young thug who had attempted to rob Kleigh came running back to him. Tron gave him his weapon back and looked at the damage to his face.

"My bad, Rello. I had to make it look real," Tron said, pulling out his wallet.

"No pain, no gain," Rello said and watched Tron count $500 and hand the money over.

"Y'all been staying low?" Tron asked, and Rello nodded his head.

"Yup. Just waiting on your call so we can take this nigga down, G."

"Word," Tron said. "Just let me work my magic, and it's gon' happen for sure."

"I wish I could work some magic on that one," Rello said, wiping his hand down on his face. "Whoo! That bitch is bad. Booty phat, nice titties, pretty face, business savvy. Man, you sure you gon' be able to stay in character? That's the type of bitch known to drive a nigga crazy."

"Niggas like me don't get pussy whipped, youngblood," Tron said with a smirk. "That's why I'm the boss, and you're the runner. All you young niggas think about is pussy."

"You ain't know? I'm a runner 'cause I runs in and out of pussy! I beats it up too!" Rello made a pull up motion with his arms and started laughing. "Nah, G, I feel you, though. But you always calling me young like you ain't only like five or six years older than me."

"In the streets, those are like dog years," Tron told him. "I'm about to shake spot. Get out of here and try not to do no stupid shit until you hear my word. Understand?"

"Loud and clear," Rello nodded.

The two did a handshake before going separate ways. Tron was telling the truth when he said he was going to check out Kleigh's spot. He went in and ordered a slice of cake and some coffee to go. When he got back to his car, he couldn't wait. He opened the small container of red velvet and broke off a piece with his fingers. The moment it hit his tongue, he knew Kleigh was right. He enjoyed it so much that he knew he would be back.

He finished eating the cake and tossed the small Styrofoam container out the window. Glancing in his rearview mirror, he saw the black Mercedes that was posted outside of the bakery. He'd been sure to park far enough away not to be detected and had kept his head down when he'd gone into the bakery. He figured that whoever was in the car was a part of Klax's entourage and was probably in charge of watching Kleigh. They were doing a pretty bad job of it because, with all that had just taken place in the alley, they hadn't budged. She also wasn't even at the bakery anymore. He shook his head, knowing that if he had wanted to harm Kleigh, it would have been all too easy. Hopefully, his next hit would be as easy. Tron grabbed his phone from his pocket and called his best shooter, Nushawn.

"NuNu," Tron said when the phone was picked up.

"What's up, Tron?"

"Are y'all in position?"

"Yeah," NuNu answered. "We planted all the devices."

"Good. Blow that bitch up."

Tron disconnected the phone and tossed it to the passenger seat. By being back in the place where he was born, he'd learned a lot about the king of Harlem. Including that not only was he a dope-dealing boss, but he played an active part in the community as well. Klax had helped rebuild a homeless shelter, put a few kids through college, and had even opened a few neighborhood recreation centers around New York. None of that did anything to sway Tron's decision to burn Klax's operation to the ground, however. In fact, all it did was give Tron more ammunition to work with. By keeping his ear to the streets the way his uncle Kyan had taught him, Tron found out that Klax was in the middle of trying to purchase an old theater and transform it into a museum of art. He was having some trouble since the council wanted to turn it into a subsidized housing division. Tron figured that he would side with neither. He had his men rig the entire building up with explosives to blow it sky-high. After a few moments, his phone rang in the passenger's seat, and he answered without looking at the screen.

"Is it done?"

"Is what done?"

Kleigh's voice caught him by surprise. He cleared his throat and sat up a little straighter.

"My bad, I thought you were somebody else," he said. "What's going on? You miss me already?"

"You wish. I was just calling to tell Sexy Chunky Peanut Butter that he can pick me up at around seven."

"OK. Send your address, so he knows where to come get you, and I will relay the message. Is there anything else you wanted to say to him?"

"Yes, there is, actually. I wanted to ask him why he saved himself in my phone as Sexy Chunky Peanut Butter."

"Because of the way you look at him."

"And how do I look at him?"

"Like you want to eat him up."

He was afraid that his bluntness had turned her off because she was quiet for a few moments. He couldn't even hear her breathing. He was about to ask if she was still there, but then she spoke up.

"I guess that's fair then," she said. "I guess since you're blunt, I can be too. I think you're fine; beyond it, actually. But that can only get you so far with a woman like me."

"A woman like you?"

"Yes, a woman like me. One that doesn't need a man for shit. Understand that I don't go on dates often, so don't waste my time. If you just want to fuck me, say that."

"Of course, I want to fuck you, but not at this particular moment. I just want you to let a nigga show you a good time. Is that too much to ask?"

"I guess no. But I want to tell you something else."

"I think you've just said a lot," Tron said, suddenly turned on.

"Well, I want to say something else. I'll let you take me out, but whatever happens tonight and after, don't get attached to me. Understand?"

"Understood."

"Perfect. I'm sending my address now."

The line went dead signifying that she had disconnected the call. His breathing was shallow, and for the first time in a while, he was thrown for a loop. In his hand, his phone vibrated once. When he looked at the screen, it was a text from her with an address. He made a mental note of it and was about to put the device in his cup holder when it rang again. That time it was NuNu.

"Hello?" he answered.

"It's done, boss," NuNu. "The building is nothing but cobblestone and ash."

"Good."

Seven o'clock came faster than Tron anticipated, but he was ready for it. He hoped that her mood wasn't changed by the news that the theater Klax was looking to acquire had been blown to pieces. It had been breaking news on every news station since it had happened.

His plan was not only to show Kleigh a great time but to dive so deeply into her mind that she wouldn't want to fish him out. She already was proving to be a tough cookie to crack, but he needed to earn her trust. A few hours before seven o'clock had hit, Kleigh sent him a message asking him to pull to the back of her building, and she would come out that way. She gave him the code to get through the gate and told him to call her when he was there. He did not ask her to elaborate. After seeing Klax's goon outside the bakery, he was positive there would be someone sitting outside of her condo too. That was also the reason he figured it would be better to tone down on his wheels. He made Kyan bring him his gray 2019 Mercedes-Benz C 300. It wasn't a Ferrari, but it was a car that could blend in, and that was what he was going for. When he pulled around the back of her building, he called her phone.

"Hello?"

"I'm out back," he said.

"OK, I'm coming down. Give me about five minutes. I'm touching up my lipstick."

"Bet."

He hung up and waited patiently for her. In exactly five minutes, he saw her come out of the tall glass doors and walk toward his car as if she owned the air around her. Even though she was walking at a normal speed, it was like she was moving in slow motion. She wore a sleeveless black tube dress that stopped just above her ankles. The dress was so simple, but her curves set the entire look off. She was so thick that he could see her backside from the front and her thighs jiggled with each step she took in her open-toe ankle strap heels. Her makeup was flawless, and she no longer rocked the long hair she had earlier that day. Instead, she'd opted to wear her natural hair in a twist out style that touched her back. Tron grabbed the rose and got out of the car so that he could get her door.

"Well, don't you clean up nice," she said with a smile.

That night, he opted for a fitted burgundy suit with diamond cuff links. He left the top buttons of the white shirt he wore under his jacket open and showcased the lion tattoo on his chest.

"I should be saying that to you. Seeing you walk out that door just took my breath away," he said, handing her the rose. "For you."

"Just one?" She raised her perfectly arched eyebrow at him but took the flower.

"I was going to get a dozen, but then I figured I'd just choose the most beautiful one instead. No point in adding others where they don't compare."

Tron noticed that her eyes lit up like stars before the corners of her lips stretched. He also noticed that she only had one dimple on the right side of her face. The smile only lasted for a few seconds after she took the rose, and he opened her door.

"You have a way with words, Tron," she told him and got in the car.

"I only speak the truth," he said, shutting her door.

He got back in the driver's seat and drove away from the condo. From the corner of his eye, he saw her get comfortable in her seat. She looked around the vehicle, and he couldn't tell if she was impressed with it.

"No 'Rari today?" she asked, leaning against her door and slightly turning to face him.

"Nah. I wanted to be inconspicuous, so to speak."

"Aaah, I get it. You must have a little girlfriend you're hiding from. You don't want her to see you out with me."

"You're on funny time, I see," Tron said with a laugh. "I don't even know the last time I had one of those."

"So you must be a player."

"I mean, I've played the field a little bit in my day, but right now, I'm just chilling. Waiting to see what God decides to blow my way."

"Blow your way, huh?"

"Yeah, blow my way," Tron said glancing at her. "And you're one to talk about hiding."

"What do you mean?" she asked with a smirk.

"The whole, 'Pick me up out back,' thing. You got a nigga you're hiding from or something? 'Cause I'm letting you know I keep a blower on me at all times."

"No!" Kleigh said, laughing. "No, I definitely do not have a boyfriend. It's my brother. He's protective of me. Overly protective."

"So why do you have to sneak out then?" Tron asked, playing dumb. "He got cameras watching you or something?"

"Worse," she told him. "He has his goons over me twenty-four seven. I'm 25 years old and still have babysitters. Ain't that crazy?"

"Goons? Your brother must be something serious," Tron said, acting like he didn't know who her brother was.

"Some people call him the king of Harlem. You may have heard of him, Klax Turner?"

"Sounds familiar," Tron faked like he was wracking his brain. "I may have heard it in passing. I just moved back here not too long ago, though, so don't be offended."

"I'm not," she said with a smile. "It's refreshing to be fresh to somebody. No . . . It's refreshing to have someone treat me like a person and not a fragile vase or some shit. Niggas usually run the other way when I get close."

"That must be why you don't go on dates like that."

"That, and the fact that I don't fuck around. I don't let niggas around me just because they want to be. So consider yourself lucky."

"I consider myself lucky every day I'm on this earth," Tron told her matter-of-factly. "A female doesn't make or break me."

When she was quiet, he turned his head to look at her, only to see that she was staring at him. There was a curious smile frozen on her face, and he returned it with one of his own. He reached over and grabbed her hand in his.

"You good over there?" he asked and caressed the top of her hand with his thumb.

"Yeah," she told him. "I'm just trying to decipher the vibe I'm getting right now. I feel like you want to be here with me, but then again, I feel like you don't care."

Tron knew the exact vibe that she was talking about. It was true that he thought she was a beautiful woman, but the fact still remained that she was the offspring of the man who had murdered his family. Naturally, his soul was repelled by Kleigh. She was nothing but a body in the way of his ultimate goal, but still, he knew he needed to tone the chilly vibe down some if he wanted to get anywhere with her.

"My bad. I don't do shit like this all the time."

"I guess we can just take baby steps together then," Kleigh suggested. "You said you just moved back. Where are you from?"

"Well, I'm from Harlem," Tron started. "But I moved upstate with my dad when I was 7."

"Why did you leave?"

"My mom died," he told her simply. "My dad just couldn't stand being here anymore, I guess."

"I'm sorry to hear that about your mom," Kleigh said, squeezing his hand slightly. "My dad passed away a few years back. He had prostate cancer."

Serves him right. I hope it was a slow, painful death, Tron thought.

"It was slow and painful," Kleigh spoke his thoughts aloud.

She was quiet for a moment, and when he looked over at her, she seemed to be in deep thought. Her jaw was tight, and her eyes were focused on the road.

"My bad. I didn't mean to fuck up the vibe," he told her, but she shook her head.

"No, it's not you. It's just . . ." She sighed. "I can tell you're a street nigga, so I'm sure you can understand what I'm about to say. It's just sometimes I wonder if my dad getting cancer was the universe's design."

"You gotta elaborate a little more on that one."

"I loved my dad dearly, but I'm not gon' be one to sit up here and act like he was a saint. Before Klax, *he* was the king of Harlem and hearing about some of the things he did used to give me nightmares. He was a very selfish man, and sometimes he had this mean streak that not even I was exempt from. So, sometimes, I wonder if him getting cancer was a way for the universe to make him pay for all of those terrible things he's done. All of the people that he hurt."

"If that's the case, don't you think the universe might do the same thing to your brother? Or you, for that matter. Blood ties never end."

"Nah," Kleigh shook her head and smiled fondly at the thought of her brother. "Klax is different. He doesn't rule by stomping the little people out, and he gives back to the community. He respected my father the way a son should, but he doesn't want to be like him. Don't get me wrong, my brother will get shit popping if you force his hand, and that's a side of him you don't want to see. But he runs Harlem with love."

"But he still sells drugs. And don't drugs kill people?"

"True, and you know that's something I used to battle with often. But I came to the conclusion that's something out of his control. The drug market is always gon' be there with or without him. My brother doesn't sell directly to fiends, and he doesn't have niggas on the corners either. His shit is way bigger than that. Ain't no money in a twenty-five-dollar bag. What the fuck is that gon' do? Fill up his gas tank? Nah. Klax's operation ain't even in Harlem. This is just the heart and soul. My father destroyed our community. Klax is just doing what he can to clean it up."

Her words simmered and sizzled in his head the rest of the drive to the Italian restaurant in downtown Manhattan called Stella's. He hoped she enjoyed pasta as much as he did because that was the place's specialty. He'd selected it from Google and was pleased to see that the place was just as beautiful in real life as it was on the web. Once he parked, he got out of the car and opened the door for her.

"Thank you," she smiled up at him and took his hand.

He liked the way she gripped it as they walked. It was like she was letting everyone know that she was with him. Or maybe it was that she was letting them know he was with her. Once they were inside the lavish restaurant, they were seated instantly because Tron had thought to call in a reservation ahead of time.

"Follow me," the hostess said.

She was an older woman, as were the majority of the people working there. He liked the atmosphere of the place. Everyone they passed smiled and welcomed them, and their server came to their table right away after they were seated.

"Hello, my name is Rosa. I'll be helping you today," the woman said with a thick accent. "May I start you off with some drinks?"

Rosa looked to be in her early forties and wore a black pants suit with an apron over it. Her long hair was in a low ponytail braid that went down her back. She got her pen and notepad out and looked at Tron.

"We'll have a bottle of your finest wine, please," Tron said, but Kleigh shook her head.

"Do you guys have Moscato? It doesn't matter the brand. I just hate the taste of bitter wine," she asked Rosa. "Oh, and some water, please."

"Of course we do," she said. "I'll go grab a bottle of it right away."

"Moscato?" Tron asked Kleigh when the server was gone and gave her a humored look.

"It's sweet, like me," she said with a wink.

"Maybe one day I can find that out for myself," he said.

"Maybe."

"From what you were saying over the phone, it's a very possible 'maybe.'"

From across the table, Kleigh batted her long eyelashes at him. He found himself staring at her lips and wondering what they would feel like wrapped around his manhood. He kept his thoughts to himself as he started to look over his menu. When Rosa came back with the wine and waters, Kleigh was ready to order.

"Can I have this lasagna dish right here," she said and pointed to the menu. "And can I make the salad that comes with it Caesar with Caesar dressing, please."

"Of course," Rosa nodded her head and jotted the order down in her notepad. "And is the garlic bread that comes with that okay with you?"

"Oh, of course! That's what makes the meal ten times better," Kleigh said.

"Perfect. And for the gentleman?"

"What I want isn't on the menu," Tron said, and a shy expression overcame Kleigh at the way he stared at her. "But I can settle for some shrimp Alfredo if you have it."

"All right. And is garlic bread okay with you, sir?"

"Definitely."

"Well, I'll go put these orders in for you."

"Thank you," the pair said in unison.

Tron took the initiative and poured them both glasses of wine. He took a small gulp of his and mentally commended Kleigh on the selection. In truth, he wasn't really a drinker, but he had to admit the Moscato was good.

"What you want isn't on the menu, is that right, Mr. Sexy Chunky Peanut Butter?" Kleigh asked as she sipped from her glass.

"You're correct," Tron said, giving her a devilish grin and placing his wine back on the table. "I could really go for a burger right now."

"Oh, you asshole," Kleigh laughed and tried to swat his hand, but he caught it.

He brought her fingers to his lips and kissed them tenderly, so tenderly that she closed her eyes and let out a happy sigh. It was then that he physically saw her let her guard down. Maybe it was the wine, but either way, he could see the progress that he was making. She'd told him a little about her brother, but no more than he could find out on the streets. He needed to dig deeper.

"Earlier today, did you really go inside and get something?"

"Yeah, I did, actually. A slice of red velvet cake."

"And?"

"It's just like you said . . . I might get addicted." Tron kissed her fingers again, and she shivered. "Now tell me one thing, why is it that you wouldn't want me to get attached to you?"

"I already told you. My brother—"

"I'm not worried about your brother."

"That's because you haven't met him."

"There isn't a nigga far or near that puts fear in my heart. So, I'm gon' ask you again. Why wouldn't you want me to get attached to you?"

"Because an attachment to me would be too complicated. I've never had a boyfriend before."

"Really?"

"Deadass. I told you, nobody comes close to me. There have been a few that tried to fuck me on the low, but I'm not going for that."

"So, you're a virgin?"

"Yes," Kleigh said and laughed at his baffled expression. "What? That's so hard to believe? I mean, of course, I've done stuff with guys, but I've never gone all the way."

"Aaah . . . I get it."

"What do you get, Tron?"

"It's not an attachment from me that concerns you. It's an attachment *to* me that you're worried about."

"What? No." Kleigh made a face and smacked her lips. "Now you're just twisting my words."

"I see your game," Tron winked and chuckled. "It's too early to think so far ahead anyways. Let's just enjoy each other's company tonight and let the cards fall where they may. If you don't want to see me again after this, that's fine."

"Okay," she said and gave him a wondrous look. "You have an old soul. I can tell by the way you speak."

"Just earlier you said I was a street nigga."

"I mean, you're that too. It's a good balance. I like it."

"Enough to stay the night with me?"

"Ummm . . ."

"I don't want nothing you don't wanna give," Tron told her truthfully. "I'm just thinking about how fast this dinner is gon' be over, and I don't know if I'll be ready to say goodbye."

After a few moments of thought, Kleigh finally nodded her head.

"Okay," she said.

By then, their food had finally come, and Kleigh still had an uncertain expression on her face, but then she stared at him, and he saw it instantly wash away. Tron grabbed his fork and fed her a bite of his food. Her eyes lit up in delight, and he fed her another. His plan had gone smoothly. As he fed her one last bite, he definitely did believe that he'd taken a deep dive into her mind. But what he didn't plan on was her doing the same to him. By the time Tron finished eating, he had lost track of how many times he had laughed. He couldn't help it. Being in her presence made the corners of his mouth touch his ears like his face was naturally arranged like that. He was confused by how at ease he was with her, and he shouldn't have enjoyed himself the way that he had, knowing that he was using her. But his eyes were still on the prize, and he'd rather his work be enjoyable than the opposite. He took care of the tab and left their waitress a hundred-dollar tip before they left. On the way to his car, Kleigh grabbed Tron by the arm to stop him.

"What's good, shorty?" Tron looked down at her and asked.

Instead of answering, Kleigh stood up on her tiptoes and kissed him on his lips. Hers were succulent, soft, and he could taste the pasta sauce on her tongue. He didn't mind it, actually. He placed his hands on her small waist and kissed her back. When she finally pulled away, she looked fondly up into his eyes.

"Sorry, I had to get that out of the way."

"And why is that?"

"Because there wouldn't even be a point in seeing you again if your kisses didn't give me butterflies."

"And what's the verdict?" Tron asked, but Kleigh just winked.

"Ask me out again, and we'll see," she said and walked to the passenger side of the car.

"Yeah, yeah," Tron said, rubbing his chin and watching her butt switch as she walked. "You know a nigga got them magic lips; stop playing. And you better not touch that door handle."

"You the controlling type?" Kleigh said, turning back to face him with her hand on her hip.

"Never that," Tron said, walking up and opening the door for her. "But I'm a real man, and I was raised old school. No woman I'm with will ever touch a door in my presence. You feel me? Just 'cause y'all worship city girls doesn't mean there aren't any gentlemen left in the world."

"I don't worship city girls. I'm a Summer Walker-type of bitch," Kleigh said, getting in the car.

"Is that right? I guess that means you need some—" Tron shut the door before he finished his sentence and grinned at the shocked look on her face. When he got in the car, he started it and posed another question. "So where to, shorty? You going back to the jailhouse or you gon' roll with me?"

"Where are you going?"

"Most likely, just back to the crib. We can Netflix and chill," he said, and when he saw Kleigh's eyebrow shoot up to the hood of the car, he chuckled. "Yo, you're bugging. Nah, like really Netflix and chill."

"Umm, I'm not sure," Kleigh said, reaching into her bag and pulling out her phone.

She must have powered it down while they were at dinner because she had to turn it on. As soon as the screen lit up, Tron could see a slew of messages come through.

"Shit," he heard her say under her breath.

"What, your man looking for you?"

"No. My brother," she said, sending a quick text and powering her device off again. "I don't even feel like dealing with him right now. That nigga thinks he's my daddy for real."

"So, I take that as you're rolling with me?"

"I guess I am," she said with a smile. "Stop by a store, though. I need to get some clothes for tomorrow."

"Bet," Tron said and pulled out of the parking garage.

Chapter 7

*"If you don't have the information you need to make
wise choices, find someone who does."*

—Lori Hill

Klax

No, I'm not home, but I'm sure you know that because
I'm sure you're there or have been there. I'm fine. Turning
my phone back off, I'll talk to you tomorrow.

Klax read his sister's text message to himself before
clenching his teeth and putting his phone back in his
pocket. He'd been trying to reach her all day after finding
out that the theater he was close to closing on had gotten
blown up. They were running the story on every news
station, and he felt as if someone had blasted him in the
chest with a shotgun. Tron had aimed for something
important to him, so Klax had no clue what dude would
go after next.

As soon as Klax found out about the theater, he rushed
over to the bakery to check on Kleigh, but Jasmine had
told him that she'd left for the day already. He then
went to her home, but no luck there either. When he
called his mother and asked if she'd seen her and she
said she hadn't, Klax began to panic. He had his people
tearing up the city looking for her, but now that she had
finally responded, he could call them off. He could hear

the attitude in her voice through the text and knew that she wasn't in any imminent danger. He wanted to be annoyed at her disappearing act, but he was too busy being relieved. She was probably hiding out with Bahli, which would explain why she didn't answer his phone call either.

"You good, boss?" Dame's voice said, invading his thoughts. Klax nodded his head and glanced over in the passenger seat in his 2019 milky-white Range Rover. The two men were parked outside of a run-down complex in Harlem people watching and plotting their next move.

"Cancel the search for my sister. But I still don't want none of these little niggas to sleep until I have a body at my feet. I'm done moving blindly in my own city. Also, tighten up security on that drop coming in on Saturday and double up at the mayor's event. I don't need this nigga fucking up both ends of my business."

"No doubt," Dame said and then gave Klax a concerned look. "You ain't answer me though, G. You good?"

"You know I ain't good," Klax answered, facing the front of the vehicle and staring out the window. "That nigga touched down and instantly started wrecking shit. I still don't know how he managed to one up me in my own shit, but this? This was the last straw. It's war, and you let everybody know that shit."

"A'ight, I'm about to hit the block," Dame said and opened the vehicle's door. "I'll let you know what the word is as soon as I have something."

After he shut the door, Klax watched him walk up the street and disappear. It was a tense time for him, and his patience was completely gone at that point. Usually levelheaded, Klax could feel the beast inside of him thrashing around, trying to get free. He couldn't help but think how hard he had worked, only for it to all blow up in his face, literally. He took the deepest breath he could before putting the Range Rover in drive. As he drove, his thoughts fell on his old man.

Coming up, all Klax wanted to be was a man equal to his father. Back in the day, Kameron's corner boys could flip twenty-five kilos in a week in Harlem. Nobody dared to run down on him on his own turf, and the respect that people had for him made Klax admire his father. However, when he learned that it wasn't respect that gave Kameron his power and that instead, it was fear, his perception changed.

Although Klax and Kleigh attended private schools, Klax could never seem to stay away from what was considered "the wrong side of town." His father hated when he left their home in the Bronx and made his way to Harlem, so he had to sneak to do so. He made a few of his lifelong connections, including Dame, by skipping school to run the streets. That was when he grew to love them and the people in them. He'd never seen a drug addict in real life until one day he saw one of his dad's corner thugs sell an eight ball in person. The addict's name was Ana Pearl, and she was only in her late twenties but looked twice her age. He remembered that she didn't have the money to pay for the drugs, so the corner boy made her suck his dick in broad daylight to cover the charges. When she was done demeaning herself, Klax watched her smoke the drugs up and pass out on the side of an apartment complex in broad daylight. It was then that he stopped seeing his father as a hero and instead, saw him as a villain. He knew even then at 16 that you couldn't force someone out of a habit, but you could help guide them. All his father wanted to do was poison their community and not spend a dollar of the profits to help rebuild it.

Since Klax was younger, he thought Harlem was the most beautiful part of New York. When he turned 18,

Kameron told him that there would be a time where he would run it. All Klax could think about was what he would do differently when the torch was passed down to him. What he should have thought about was how his father had gotten to be the head honcho in the first place, but he never cared. That same carelessness was what had caused the current problems unfolding before him. If he had known about his father's moves, then Klax would have gotten Tron's head blown back a long time ago. However, since it was too late, he figured he'd do the next best thing. Get as much information about Tron as he could. And there was only one person who he knew could answer some of his questions.

It was a little after ten at night when he pulled into the curved driveway of his childhood home. The light in the front room was still on, and he knew his mom, Dorian Turner, was still awake. He used his key to open the door and heard the alarm system start to go off but deactivate in seconds.

"I meant to turn that off," Dorian said, walking down a long hallway from the kitchen that led to the front door. "I had a feeling that you were gon' make your way over here. Come hug your mama."

"What's up, Mama?" Klax said and hugged his mom's short frame.

Dorian was a gorgeous woman in her late forties, but if she were to tell you her age, you'd think she was lying. Not only was she fit, but there wasn't a wrinkle in sight on her smooth, light brown skin. She kept the dark brown hair on her head dyed to hide the grays and stayed on a strict vegan diet. Kleigh was the spitting image of her.

"Come on back. I'm in the kitchen." She waved for him to follow her back to where she came from. "I made some gumbo if you want a bowl before I put it away."

"You already know I'ma smash that," Klax said, feeling himself instantly get hungry.

Dorian was the best cook he knew, and he didn't just think that because she was his mother. Kleigh may have had the magic touch when it came to desserts, but his mother had a special kind of gift in the kitchen. She put a piece of her soul in all of her food, and Klax honestly couldn't think of anything she made that he didn't eat.

"How'd you know I was gon' end up over here?" he asked curiously when they reached the large kitchen.

He noticed that his mother had redecorated slightly since the last time he was here a few weeks before. The glass dining room table had been replaced with a wooden one, and the wall décor was all different. The light blue walls had been painted a pastel peach. He smirked to himself recalling that was the color she wanted it to be before the original white walls were painted blue. However, Kameron refused to have an almost-pink kitchen. The floors were still wooden, but the island in the middle of the kitchen had been expanded so more people could be seated at it. Klax was happy to see that although his mom was still hiding out in the house, she was keeping herself busy. He sat down in one of the stools at the island and watched his mother hook up a bowl of seafood gumbo for him.

"I watched the news earlier, and I'm glad I did because I wasn't going to," she said bustling around the kitchen. "I'd just done my Pilates and was about to lie down when the news anchor said there was an explosion. And when I saw it was that theater you had your sights on, I felt my spirit crumble just like that building! I knew I would see you sometime today. You wanna talk about it?"

"Not really," Klax said dryly.

"Mmm," Dorian noted and set his hot bowl of gumbo in front of him. "You might not want to talk about it, but I can see the rage boiling under the surface just by looking at you. Don't go out there and do nothing stupid, boy, you hear me? There are a lot of other places you can put your museum. Shit, you can buy some land and build it from the ground up if you want to. This was probably some stupid-ass kids."

"It wasn't."

"If not, then who?"

"I was actually hoping you could help me out with that," Klax said and saw a look of bewilderment overcome her.

"Me?"

"Yeah. Quiet as kept, the shit that happened at the theater ain't the only thing that's been going on around here. I had to let Big Tony go."

"Big Tony?" Dorian's eyes grew wide. "He worked for your father for years!"

"Yeah, well, I guess tenure doesn't bring loyalty, now, does it? He tried to sell out and get me caught up. I had to do what I had to do."

"Well, good riddance then. Enough snakes are crawling around. You don't need them in your own camp."

"I agree," Klax said, taking a big bite of the hot gumbo. When he finished chewing, he glanced up at her. "Does the name Sunny Walker ring a bell?"

At the sound of the name, Dorian looked as if she'd just seen a ghost. She stopped wiping the counter and furrowed her brow at Klax. Her mouth opened, but then closed instantly like she didn't know what to say. When no words found her, she just closed her eyes and shook her head.

"What's that for? You know him, don't you?"

"I should have known this day would come," she said with a sigh and a small shoulder shrug. "Yes, I know him. Back in the day, *everybody* knew Sunny Walker."

"Because he was the kingpin of Harlem?"

"Yes," Dorian nodded. "He *was,* anyway. But that was before your daddy took over."

"You mean before he murdered Sunny's wife and daughter?"

"Don't you sit there and act like you don't know the laws of the streets. Your father tried to be reasonable with Sunny about a partnership. But Sunny wanted no part in the new Harlem your father was trying to build. And, well, after that, your father took matters into his own hands. If it's not given to you, you take it."

"Mama, I love you, but the moves of your dead husband are coming to bite me in the dick. I need to know everything you know about Sunny Walker and his son."

"His son?" Dorian asked. "You think . . . You think Sunny Walker's son is behind all of this?"

"Last night at the club, I got a little visit from a man claiming to be Sunny Walker's son. He said he was coming back for his rightful place on the throne."

"I told your father to finish the job when he had the chance. It wasn't like him to leave loose ends." Dorian shook her head. "He was the one who intervened with the killing of that boy. He told your uncle Johnny to let the kid live. To let him watch his entire family bleed in front of him."

"Did Sunny die?"

"No," she shook her head. "I was a nurse for the trauma unit back then. I saw them rush Sunny into surgery to treat the gunshot wound he suffered to the head. If I had been able to get close enough, I would have pulled the plug on him myself. Before I ever saw him again, he was gone. But I heard that he survived the surgery."

"And Dad never thought to handle that?"

"No. I think it made Kameron feel powerful . . . to take down New York's crime family and become better than they ever did. In his mind, he'd broken Sunny down past the point of revenge, and I don't think for one second he felt Sunny would come for him."

"And I guess he figured Sunny's son would just forget about what happened to his family?" Klax pushed away his bowl of food in front of him, suddenly not having an appetite. "Your husband was something else; you know that? His problem was that he thought he was invincible . . . when really, he was just stupid as fuck."

"I will not let you bad-mouth your father in this house!"

"The same one who cheated on you with the house-keeper for years? We're talking about this same house, right?" Klax said glaring at her for defending his deceased father. "I spent years living in the shadow of a man who was just the used up shell of one. He stole Sunny's spot for the power, and that's it. After he died, I swore that I wouldn't run things the way he did. He was a fool sitting on a mound of gold, but I'm a true king sitting on diamonds. And I won't let his dumb mistakes ruin me. So, you need to let me know where I can find Sunny so I can dead this shit once and for all."

"And how are you gon' do that? That man is gon' take one look at you and try to blow your head off."

"That's a risk I'm gon' have to take. Not too long ago, I was just in the car and declared a street war. But after talking to you, that shit ain't even worth it. The blood that is running in my veins is the reason for this feud, so I'm going to use it to form a truce."

"A *truce?* Your father would never—"

"Exactly," Klax cut her off and stood up from the table. "At his oldest age, my father couldn't measure up to the man I am today. Unless necessary, I prefer to keep the blood off the streets."

"And if it's inevitable?"

"You just answered your own question." Klax went around the island to kiss her forehead. "I'll call soon, Mama."

"Wait!" Dorian said when he started to walk away.

"What's up?" When he turned around, he saw a look of concern in her eyes.

"About your sister, loosen up the reins on her a bit," Dorian said. "She feels like her life is a damn prison with you always watching her every move. She isn't a preschooler who needs an escort wherever she goes."

Klax knew that Kleigh often called their mom to vent about things. For the most part, Dorian agreed with his reasons behind why he was the way he was. She rarely said anything to him about the way he was when it came to his sister's safety. Any other time, he might have been willing to come to a compromise, but it just wasn't the right time.

"If you think that while all this is happening that I'm gon' do that, you're out of your mind. You just spoke about the laws of the streets, and isn't one of them 'an eye for an eye'? The most I can do is tell my soldiers to fall back more into the background," Klax said and turned his back on her. "But just know both you and her always have a few people with y'all."

"All Kleigh is going to do is find ways to hide and get away from you, Klax," she sighed. "You're gon' push her away."

"After all of this shit is over, you have my word. I *will* loosen up a bit, a'ight?"

"OK," Dorian said, taking a few quick steps to embrace her son. When she pulled back, she looked up into his handsome face and placed a gentle hand on his cheek. "You know what? You were right about one thing."

"What's that?"

"Your father couldn't measure up to the man you are today. You've always been so smart, and I'm proud of you for that. But just be careful, you hear me? Your father may have been a lot of things, but I would be lying if I told you I didn't love him until the day he died. That's a pain that I don't want to relive, understand?"

"I got you, Mama," he said. "Ain't nothing gon' happen to me."

He left her house and started toward his own home not too far down the way when he felt his phone going off. He almost ignored it, but something told him to see who was calling. When he looked, he saw that the caller ID read "Bakery." He raised his eyebrow. It was too late for anyone to be there, and he doubted that his sister was there.

"Hello?"

"Klax! Klax, i-it's me, Jasmine. Please help me. They h-have guns."

He sat up straight in the driver's seat when he heard the fear in her voice.

"Who? Who has guns?"

"I don't know. T-they told me to—"

"Gimme this shit," Klax heard a voice in the background say before someone else got on the phone. "What up, bitch-ass nigga?"

"Yo, who the fuck is this?" Klax barked.

"Come find out for ya'self," the voice said. "The deal is you show up alone and willingly, and then you take me to your main stash spot."

"You must be dumb."

"Nah, but I know how much your sister loves this little bakery y'all have here. If you don't show up, we not just gon' blow it up like we did that theater. We gon' send this bitch up in flames with the girl in it. You have an hour."

Click!

"Fuck!" Klax bellowed and hit the steering wheel of his vehicle. "Shit!"

If something happened to Turner's Bakery, Kleigh would never forgive him. Not only that, but he couldn't have Jasmine's blood on his hands. Quiet as kept, she was special to him. Kleigh didn't know it, but before his father took him completely under his wing, the two of them had a thing. He would have fallen in love with her if he hadn't fallen in love with the streets first. He always figured he would have time to act on those feelings again, but not until he had the time to settle down.

He mulled over his options for a few moments before realizing that he only had one. He had to go. Before he pulled off, however, he drove around to the far back of the house to the shed. He got out of the car and used a key on his key ring to undo the lock. He rarely had to go there, but because he wasn't close enough to his own home, what was there would have to do. He swung the door to the shed open and stepped inside. To anyone else, all they would have seen were the old yard tools his father used to do work with, but Klax looked past all of that. He walked to the back wall and moved a lawnmower and blower out of the way. Placing his hand on the wall, he applied pressure to it and slid it to the side. It was a trick wall that his father had installed to hide what he really kept in the shed: guns, guns, and more guns. Klax loaded up on everything he needed, including a bulletproof vest. He then checked every clip and strapped each firearm to his body before sliding the wall back and locking the shed up again. If it were a storm they wanted, then he would bring a hurricane.

He went back to his vehicle and sped away from his mom's house. Klax didn't have a game plan, but what he did know was that by the end of the night, he would still be the only one who knew where his main stash spot was.

It took him thirty minutes flat to get to the bakery. He parked in the back alley. He was sure that dude on the phone wasn't alone, but that didn't mean anything to him. He'd gone to battle as a lone wolf before and had turned all of his opponents to slaughtered sheep. Positive that the white shirt he wore was going to be stained with the blood of his enemies when he was done, Klax got out of the vehicle. As he walked, he screwed the silencer on the pistol in his hand. He eased his way toward the brick building, making sure to steer clear of the surveillance camera. He waited for it to swivel to the other side before he did a dash to the back door of the bakery and entered through the kitchen. The lock had been broken, and Klax figured that was how they'd gotten inside.

Already prepared for whatever, he wasn't shocked to see that there was someone standing patrol at that door, but his back had been turned when Klax came in. The man was in all black and whipped around at the sound of someone coming up behind him and tried to reach for his gun. He was too slow. Klax hit him with a quick jab to his esophagus, and when the man choked on his own breath, Klax put a bullet between his eyes. His head snapped back from the clean shot, and Klax caught him before he fell on the counter and lay his dead body down gently. One of the reasons was because he didn't want to alarm the other intruders, and the second was because he didn't want to hear his sister's grief about having a dead man on her counters. He removed the mask from the man's face and saw that he didn't recognize him.

Leaving him where he was, Klax crept through the dark kitchen toward the front of the bakery where he could hear faint voices. He moved as silently as he could until he was able to get a good look at his opponents. They were all hiding in the shadows with their guns drawn, waiting for him to show up. Had he come in through the main entrance of the bakery, they would have surrounded him. He counted four total. One of them had a mask over his face, but his thick, short dreads were sticking straight in the air.

"Where this nigga at?" Bad Hair said.

Klax knew instantly that he was the one he'd talked to over the phone. The fact that they were defiling a family business with not only their presence but their thirst to see him dead set him off. Klax aimed his weapon at his first victim, who was hiding behind the cash register.

Pfft!

The bullet caught the goon straight in his temple and made the other side of his head smack the register. Knowing he'd given his position away, Klax aimed his gun again and took out the man closest to the front entrance before doing the same to the one hiding underneath a table. Mr. Bad Hair tried to turn around and fire his gun at Klax. The bullet hit him in the chest but was caught by the vest he was wearing. He was so amped up on adrenaline that the power of the bullet barely slowed him down. Before the goon could fire again, Klax punched him once in the jaw, knocking him back. Klax then grabbed him by the wrist and twisted it as hard as he could.

"Aah!" the goon shouted.

The gun in his hand dropped to the floor, but Klax continued twisting until he heard the bone crack. He was still shouting in pain when Klax sent the butt of his pistol smashing into the side of the goon's head.

"The fuck was y'all thinking?" Klax said and kicked him in his mouth with the tip of his Jordan 13 when he fell to the ground. "You know who I am, right?"

"F-fuck you," the man on the floor stammered with blood pouring from his mouth, and Klax kicked him in the ribs. "Uuugh!"

"You shot me, little nigga," Klax said, touching the hole in his shirt. "For that, I'm gon' grant you a couple of more minutes of life. Tron sent you?"

"You *know* who sent me, bitch," the goon said glaring up at Klax with glossy eyes.

"I have a good guess," Klax said. "But I'm looking for confirmation."

"You might as well kill me now. 'Cause you ain't getting shit outta me," the goon said and broke into a fit of bloody coughs.

Klax, not one to beg, did as he asked. He pointed the gun down and turned the goon's head into pastrami. He clenched and unclenched the hand that wasn't holding the gun. His chest was on fire, but he would have rather the bullet hit there than to put a hole in the bakery wall.

"Mmmm! Mmmm!"

He heard the muffled sound of someone coming from the back. He'd almost forgotten about Jasmine and rushed to where the noise was coming from. He found her bound and gagged in the back office. Beads of sweat plagued her forehead, and her eyes had a look of frozen terror in them. When he cut her free, she clung to him and sobbed into his neck. Klax didn't know what to do, so he just held on to her as tightly as she was holding him.

"You good, shorty," he assured her. "Everything is good. I handled that."

As she cried, he reached for the phone in his pocket and sent a text to his cleaner team to get there ASAP. He put the phone back and rubbed Jasmine's back, trying to sooth the fear out of her. He figured right then wasn't the time to inform her to keep what had happened there that night between the two of them.

Instead, he decided to take her home. He told her he would take her to get her car in the morning because he didn't think she was in the right state of mind to drive. Klax helped her to her feet and led her through the kitchen and out the back door. Seeing the busted lock as he passed made him shake his head. It had been the first time in history that someone had been that bold with him. Klax didn't want to admit it, but Tron's recklessness made him worried about the mayor's birthday event.

"What were you even doing here so late, Jas?" Klax asked her and began to drive off.

When he pulled out of the alley, he saw a white van pull into it. It had only been about fifteen minutes, but he was pleased to see his people on their jobs. He didn't care what they did with the bodies of Tron's people, as long as they got them out of the bakery.

"I was there late tonight making sure that everything was good for the event tomorrow, and I must have fallen asleep," Jasmine said, shaking her head. "Next thing I know, I'm waking up to a gun pointed in my face."

The visual caused Klax's jaws to clench. Had he walked in and seen Jasmine's body on the ground, he didn't know how he would have felt. His ornery expression didn't go unnoticed by Jasmine. She reached over and placed a hand on his leg, squeezing it gently.

"Hey, I'm good, just like you said."

"I just keep thinking about what if something *had* happened to you."

"It did, but I'm here," she said. "On the bright side, it's nice to know that you still care about me."

"I never stopped caring," Klax said glancing over at her. "You should know that."

"Then why—" Jasmine started, but Klax cut her off already knowing what she was going to say.

"Look what happened tonight. You know why we can't be together."

"We aren't together, and look what happened tonight," she shot back, using his own words against him. "I love you, Klax. You know that. Do you understand how hard it is hiding that? Every day, it's like I'm living a lie. When Kleigh talks about you, I have to pretend like I know nothing about you. When you used to come to the bakery all the time, I had to act like just being in your presence didn't bother me. And now, you barely come in, and I miss seeing your face. It makes me feel crazy! Do you know how that feels?"

Klax wanted to do anything and say anything to make the hurt in her voice go away. However, there were no words he could offer to ease the pain she felt because he still couldn't give her what she wanted. However, he knew how she felt. Being around her, he always felt like an invisible magnetic force was pulling him to her, which was why he had to stop going into the bakery so much. Whenever he had a moment to imagine what life would be like once he could sit and enjoy it, it would always be with her. The hardest thing to do was deny his heart what it desired, but he had to do it one more time.

"I'm sorry, Jas," he said finally.

"Yeah, I *bet* you are," she scoffed and crossed her arms. "Just take me home."

"You sure you don't want to come to my spot?"

"Whoever those niggas were back there didn't want me. They wanted you. I'll take my chances in my own shit."

They didn't say another word to each other the rest of the ride to her apartment. Before she got out, she gathered her things, and Klax watched her. He wanted to tell her to stay, but no changed behavior would immediately follow, so he bit his tongue.

"I'm still gon' have somebody come through and post up tonight, OK?"

"Do whatever it is you feel you gotta do," she said and opened the door.

"Don't be like that."

"It's not me being like anything," she said and made to get out, but paused. "You know, it's hard for me to let another man even get close to me."

"You got a man?" Klax asked, not hearing any of the other words she said, and she rolled her eyes.

"No, I don't, and *that's* the problem. I've been sitting around for the past two years waiting for you. The moment I think something is getting too serious, I back off, because none of these niggas compare to you. But you know what? I'm *done* doing that. You made your choice, and I'm finally making mine. I hope the streets keep you warm at night."

Without a final word, she slammed the door to the Range Rover and headed for the lit up stairs of her apartment complex. Klax sat there watching her, wishing that it was regret he felt. Because then, he would have gotten out of the car and chased after her. Instead, he did exactly what he said he would and called someone to stand watch over her apartment complex.

Chapter 8

"The way they leave tells you everything."
—*Anonymous*

Adonis

Bzzz! Bzzz! Bzzz!

Adonis ignored the phone vibrating on his office desk. The cushioned desk chair he was sitting in was pushed back and swiveled to the side. His face was to the ceiling as he was relishing a feeling of pure bliss.

"Oooh, shit, girl. Work that mouth," he moaned.

He tightened his grip on the handful of hair he had and guided the young woman's head up and down on his shaft. He felt her full pink lips mixed with her tongue action sucking and knew that he was close to shooting all of his nut sack down her throat.

Bzzz! Bzzz! Bzzz!

His phone began to go off again, and he tried to ignore it so that he could reach his climax. He grabbed the back of the woman's head with both of his hands and made it bob quickly until he felt an electric shock shoot through his body.

"*Shit!*" Adonis said and felt his body go limp in the chair.

Bzzz! Bzzz! Bzzz!

"You gonna get that?" the woman asked.

She stood up, and Adonis watched her adjust herself before taking a seat on his desk. He grabbed the phone and finally peeped who was blowing him up. It was Klax. He hurried up and answered before it stopped vibrating. Klax never called more than once, so whatever it was, it had to have been important.

"What up, G?"

"Damn, nigga, you got me blowing you up like a bitch."

"My bad," Adonis said and glanced up at the pretty, brown-skinned queen smiling down at him. "Shit just got a little hectic in the office. What's the word, though? I heard about the theater. That's all bad, man."

"Yeah, I know. And because I don't need nothing else like that to happen, I need you to use your connects to find out some information for me."

"No doubt. What you need?"

"I need to know any and everything you can dig up about Arnold Walker and LaTron Walker."

"Wait. Ain't that what ole boy from the club said his name was?"

"Yup. Make that happen for me. And next time I call, answer."

"Got you."

Click.

Adonis placed the phone back on his desk and patted the woman on her thick thigh.

"I think Alex might need his assistant back," he told her.

"When are you going to tell Klax about us?"

"Why would I do that?" Adonis asked, making a face. "What am I supposed to say? That I'm dicking down his little sister's best friend? Bahli, be for real. You know what this is, just like I do. Plus, I'm engaged. You and I can't go any further than these little 'office visits.'"

Bahli rolled her eyes and stood up from the desk. Adonis had to admit, she looked good in yellow, and the way her dress hugged that shape of hers almost made him hard again. But he needed to focus on what Klax needed him to do, and that meant she had to leave. No distractions.

"You get on my damn nerves," she said, smacking her lips. "You know damn well that white girl ain't gon' be enough for you. She probably can't even take dick like me."

Adonis found himself grinning, even though he didn't want to. Bahli's confidence was one of the things that had turned him on about her. When he got her the job as the assistant to one of his partners, he had no idea things would end up with them sexing multiple times a week in his office. He would never admit it to her, but he was quite addicted to her loving. In a perfect world, he probably would have swept her off her feet, but being with Jessica meant more growing opportunities for his career.

"Here you go with this shit," he said, shaking his head. "You better go before Alex starts looking for you."

"Oh, don't worry; he's not," she said with a wink over her shoulder. "The two of you have a few things in common. Right now, he's in the out of order men's bathroom on the third floor with that pretty new attorney. I'm supposed to be available to tell his wife that he's in a meeting if she calls."

"Well, you better get to it, then, before Amber does one of her famous pop-ups."

"You're right," Bahli said giggling. "That bitch is crazy."

She blew him a kiss and left the office, gently closing the door behind her. Once she was gone, Adonis went to work to find the information Klax had asked him about. The rest of his day consisted of making phone calls and doing thorough research on his laptop. By the end of his day, he had found out more than enough on both parties and knew that his right hand would be pleased. He shot Klax an email before he left the office to head home. Jessica had made her "famous" tuna casserole, so Adonis wanted to make sure he had time to stop and grab something good to eat before he walked through the doors.

Adonis knew that Jessica wasn't the woman who fit his rib, but she fit his budget, and that's just what it was. She was smart, sexy, ambitious, and overall, a pretty good woman. However, the obvious differences between them had always proven to be quite the hurdle. Jessica was born with a silver spoon in her mouth, while Adonis had to fight his way up and earn his spot. He knew that wasn't her fault, but it was a part of him that she would never be able to understand. Actually, she didn't even try to understand; instead, she tried to mold him into the man that she saw fit for herself. In many different ways, she asked him to forget his roots. Many times, she told him to stay away from Klax, his brother and his best friend. In the beginning, he had been so wrapped around her finger because he couldn't believe a woman of her stature wanted to be with him. He had swayed away from his hood roots and began to turn into something that he didn't recognize. Thankfully, he caught himself. Klax was the one person in the world who had stood by his side when nobody else dared to. Klax had pulled him out of many burning hot fires and had even footed the bill for him to go to college and get his law degree. He would never turn his back on him, so their relationship was just something Jessica would have to deal with.

The drive home was peaceful. Adonis stopped at his favorite burger joint and was chewing while bobbing his head to Future's voice blasting from his speakers. The sun was still up as he pushed his sleek black Audi R8 through the streets of New York. Unlike Klax, he'd actually grown up in Harlem. So to go from barely having food to eat every day to live the lavish life he could as an adult was a blessing. He couldn't imagine ever going back to that; therefore, every day, he strived to be a better man than he was the day before.

Once he got home, he parked his car next to his fiancée's white Lexus truck in the parking garage. He looked in the rearview mirror and wiped the corners of his mouth to remove any telltale evidence of the burger. It wasn't that Jessica was a bad cook because she wasn't. However, he was used to a different kind of menu than she was. A menu that he didn't trust her to prepare for him without sitting in the kitchen with his mom first for a few lessons.

When he reached the door to his tenth-floor sky view condo, he paused when he heard voices coming from the other end. He knew it wasn't the TV because he heard Jessica's voice mingled in the conversation. Adonis hadn't been expecting company, and Jessica surely didn't tell him that they were having anyone over. He reached behind his back, under his jacket, and placed his hand around the handle of the Ruger tucked in his pants before he opened the door.

"Honey!" Jessica gushed from the well lit kitchen when she saw him enter.

Her wide smile let him know that there was no immediate danger in the large one-bedroom condo, and he let the gun go. He still didn't climb off the edge, however. He noticed that she was dressy in a skirt, a nice blouse, and stockings. Sitting at the circle table in the dining room were two men that he didn't recognize. Both were Caucasian, wearing suits and fake smiles on their faces. One wore his blond hair cut short, had dark brown eyes, and had three permanent lines on his square forehead. The other had jet-black hair that was slightly disheveled and brown eyes. Adonis only had to take one look at them to know what they were. Feds.

"Baby, you didn't tell me we were having company tonight," Adonis said and let her take his briefcase from his hands. "What's the occasion?"

"That right there with the blond hair is Detective Hanes, and that's his partner, Detective Terry. These nice gentlemen just wanted to have a few words with you; that's all." She said it like it was no big deal. "Sit down. We were waiting for you to join us before we ate."

"Your wife-to-be tells us she makes a mean tuna casserole," Detective Hanes said.

"Yeah, she does," Adonis said but didn't budge from where he was standing. "I'm sorry, I guess I'm just wondering why two feds are in my home? And why my *fiancée* would let them in."

"You got something to hide?" Detective Terry said, raising his brow at him.

"Do I?"

Adonis gave them both hard looks. He couldn't believe that Jessica would welcome two federal agents in the home where he kept private information. He shot her a look, but she ignored it as she went to make everyone's plates.

"Honey, they just want to ask you a few questions; that's it."

"Okay, what are the questions?" Adonis asked and made a motion with his hands as if to tell them to make it snappy.

"I guess we can make this quick and painless," Detective Hanes said with a smirk. "It's our understanding that you are good friends with a man named Kevin Turner?"

"What about it?"

"Well, we have reason to believe that he's been involved with quite a few illegal dealings around the state of New

York. Even a drug syndicate. Do you have any information about that?"

"Not only is Mr. Turner my friend, but he is my client. I'm sure you know that falls under client confidentiality. I'm not at liberty to speak about any matter concerning Mr. Turner with you or anyone else."

"We had a feeling you were going to say that," Detective Terry said. "And that's why we took the liberty to do some digging of our own. How does a man like you, who comes from a slum in Harlem, find yourself able to afford an education at New York Law School? Who footed that bill?"

"If you did all that digging, then you know the answer to that."

"So, Kevin Turner paid for you to go to school? How do you think he came across a pretty penny like that?"

"I'm sure you know who his father was. Kevin comes from a family of money."

"Drug money."

"That has never been a fact or proven," Adonis said not missing a beat. "The Turners have always had a part in many lucrative businesses all around the state of New York. But I guess when you're a white man who grew up with less than a black, the only way that could be is if drugs are involved, right? Get the fuck out of my house."

"Honey," Jessica stepped into the dining room and tried to calm him. "These men are just trying to help. You know that theater just got blown up, and these detectives are just doing their job. They think that Kevin did it because the state wasn't going to approve his purchase of the property. You know my daddy is on the council, and when the detectives questioned him, I told them you would be happy to cooperate in the investigation."

"You did *what?* You must be stupid," Adonis looked at her like she was a smashed spider on the bottom of his shoe.

"W-what? Don't speak to me like that."

"There ain't nothing else to speak about," Adonis said to the detectives. "Y'all can go and try to dig up whatever lies you can find on my client."

"Best friend," Detective Hanes said.

"That too," Adonis agreed.

The men, leaving their casseroles untouched, stood up and walked toward the door Adonis had opened for them. He glared at the amused expressions on their faces and stood back so that they could pass. Detective Terry stopped in front of Adonis and sized him up for a moment.

"You do know that if we connect drug money to your tuition, your license will be revoked. You won't be able to practice law anywhere in the country, let alone New York," Detective Terry warned.

"Not worried about it," Adonis responded.

The detective gave him a smirk before exiting with his partner. When they were gone, Adonis let the heavy door slam shut before he shot rounds with his eyes at Jessica. The anger in his gut was growing by the second, and he could tell that she truly felt that she had done nothing wrong by the look of annoyance on her face. He knocked the two plates of food off the table and sent them crashing into the wall.

"What the fuck, Jess?" he shouted. "What the fuck are you on? Why did you just have feds in my crib?"

"Now, why did you go and do that?" she asked and went to get a towel. "I told you why they were here. They needed to ask you some questions about Kevin."

"And you *really* thought that I would give them any kind of information about my best friend?"

"Yes, I did. Especially now that I know he was the one to put you through law school. Why didn't you tell me that?"

"Because that's not your business!"

"Now, it *is* my business! Especially if you can get your license to practice law revoked! You and I both know that Kevin is no good."

"No good to whom? You and your councilman daddy? Do you think his slate is squeaky clean? I bet you right now I can locate a few payouts under his belt in less than an hour. Don't fucking play with me like this, yo. You're really buggin'."

"*I'm* 'bugging'? Who *are* you right now?"

"The same man that you refuse to see. I'm *black,* in case you forgot," Adonis told her.

"I know you're black. Don't insult me like that. But I think you should call those detectives back and tell them what they need to know before this gets any wo—"

"Fuck you," Adonis cut her off.

"*Excuse me?*"

"I didn't stutter. I said, *fuck* you."

"Don't speak to me like that! I refuse to marry a man who disrespects me."

"You must be stupid as hell to think I'm still gon' marry you after this," Adonis told her in a disgusted manner. "Get your shit and get the fuck out of my spot. *All* your shit, 'cause you ain't coming back."

"W-wait. Adonis, baby." Jessica tried to grab his arm, but he snatched it away. "Please don't do this. I love you, and I want to be with you, baby."

"No, you don't. You want to be with one of the top lawyers in the state. You and your daddy want to control me. You don't see me as a black man, and you sure as hell don't understand me as one. Letting motherfuckin' feds in my home like you pay a bill. Bitch, you must be out of your white-ass mind. Matter of fact, I'll have your things mailed to you. But you gotta go right now. Period. I don't even wanna look at you."

By the time he finished speaking, Jessica was a pool of tears. Her sobs made it difficult for her to speak, and Adonis couldn't make out anything that she was saying. Even if he could, he wouldn't care because she had to go. She clung to him as he grabbed her purse and car keys. He dragged her to the front door and threw the purse and keys into the hallway. Then he looked down at her pitiful face and saw that her long, blond hair was sticking to her cheeks because of her tears, but he had no sympathy for her. She had crossed the line. There was no way that she could ever be his family asking him to betray his family. She had to get X'd out of his life.

"Let me go," he told her.

"If you make me leave, I'm going to the police, and I'm going to tell them that you beat me," she threatened.

"Good luck with that. You of all people should know I have cameras throughout this condo. The only thing the police will see is a crazed and demented woman who can't handle rejection."

"Please, Adonis, I love you. Please don't do this."

"Just go, Jessica. You're embarrassing yourself."

When she realized that begging wasn't getting her anywhere, she released him and stepped into the hallway. She tried to collect her dignity and pick up her things. In the time it took to stand back up, fire had replaced the saddened look in her blue eyes.

"My father was right about you. Once trash, always trash. I was the best thing that ever happened to you. I hope that when they take Kevin down, they take you wi—"

He slammed the door in her face before she could finish speaking. He didn't care about anything she was talking about. All he wanted to do was warn Klax that the Feds were watching him and to watch his steps at the mayor's birthday dinner that evening. He grabbed his phone from his briefcase and made the call.

"Bro?" Adonis said as soon as Klax picked up the phone. "What you on right now?"

"Just getting ready to handle some business."

"Word, I feel it. I just wanted to give you a heads-up. The Feds have eyes on you. They think you had something to do with that building getting blown up. So only move smart, a'ight?"

"I figured as much, and you know I move like a smooth operator, baby boy."

"You so corny," Adonis said, feeling his mood lighten a little bit. "A'ight, I just wanted to make sure that you're sharp on your toes."

"Good looking, but aye, let me holler at you later, bet?"

"Yep."

Adonis disconnected the call, and it was then that he realized the mess he made in his usually spotless condo. He was glad then that he had chosen the one with wooden floors because that nasty tuna casserole would have been hell to clean out of any carpet. He groaned and headed for the hallway closet to get a towel to clean it up and hoped that Jessica wouldn't make her way back there that night.

Chapter 9

"Worry is interest paid on trouble before it is due."
—William R. Inge

Kleigh

The night was still young, and Kleigh found herself moving around the mayor's dinner like a chicken with her head cut off. The banquet hall had been set up elegantly, and everyone who was anyone was in attendance. They were all sipping or munching on something while fraternizing with each other or dancing. Kleigh was doing neither. She was supposed to be enjoying the event, not working, but she could not help it. Not when her name was on the line. She kept going back in the kitchen to check on the extra cakes they were baking just in case they ran out of the ones they'd made at the bakery.

"Girl, if you don't get your ass out of this kitchen!" Eddy shoo'd her away the last time she'd gone back to the kitchen. He was dressed in his baker's attire with his hair pulled back. "Back here in a damn ball gown looking lost and out of place."

"I'm just making sure everything is going all right. You're back here by yourself."

Eddy turned his head side to side as if he were looking for something before glancing back at her. He gave her a wide-eyed look like if she didn't get out of his face, he was going to pop her one.

"Kleigh, I know damn well you see all these people back here. If I need help with something—which I won't—I will ask. Okay? Now, get out there and mingle. You might meet your Prince Charming."

Kleigh bit her tongue and swatted Eddy on his arm when he playfully pushed her to the exit. With a small huff, she did what he asked and went back out to the party. She recognized a lot of faces just due to the fact of the bakery being a pretty popular place in town, but that didn't mean she wanted to speak to them. She thought back to Eddy's last words, "*Prince Charming.*" She smiled to herself as she walked over to a man holding a tray of champagne flutes and took one.

"Thank you," she said.

"You're welcome, ma'am," the young man said and eyed her up and down in her Vera Wang ball gown. "The color red suits you. You look beautiful."

She smiled again and walked away. She had to admit, she was in a pretty good mood. Not only did she look good, but she smelled amazing. She'd spent a little extra time on her makeup that night, and she had gotten her long hair done in a silk press. After her date with Tron, even the air around her seemed a little warmer. He just did something good for her spirit. After having dinner the night before, she had gone back to his place despite being skeptical about it. Still, the last place she had wanted to be was in front of Klax's face after ignoring him, so she went. Tron was nothing short of a gentleman, and the two of them stayed up the entire night talking about sweet nothings. She replayed a conversation from the night before in her head . . .

"So, who are you?" she asked with her cheek rested on his chest.

The two were cuddled under the covers of his bed with a movie playing quietly in the background. Her hand gently rubbed his bare chest as she waited to feel the vibrations given off from his vocal cords. She hadn't really snuggled with a man before, so the fact that she was so comfortable doing so with him was beyond her.

"What do you mean by that?"

"Like, I see who you are on the surface, but I know that's just who you want me to see."

"So you're saying I'm putting up a façade?"

"No," she giggled. "I'm saying that I want to dive a little deeper, that's all. You know what I do, but I don't know what you do. It must be something big, right? For you to have the cars you have, and this is a pretty nice place you live in too. I'm not one into artwork, but I can tell the paintings you have all over cost a pretty penny."

"Observant, I see," he said. "But it doesn't matter what I do."

"Why doesn't it?"

"Because it just doesn't. What I do isn't who I am."

Kleigh smacked her lips. "Yup, I figured it out. You're really a street nigga."

"You keep saying that. Why?" Tron laughed.

"Because I heard my brother use that line on a few females when I was growing up. I'm not judging you. Shit, you have to get it how you live."

"Is that right?" Tron said, looking down at her.

"Yup," she said, raising her head to look up at him. "I'm not gon' judge you for that as long as you have a plan. You can't live the street life forever, unless you're willing to die for it."

"That's what my pops tells me. He wants me to take his business one day," Tron said dryly.

"And what's wrong with that?"

"It ain't lucrative enough for my taste. He had another business awhile ago that was more my speed, but he lost it."

"I'm sorry to hear that," Kleigh genuinely told him. "But we live in a world full of endless possibilities. Just because one door closes doesn't mean another won't open."

"Look at you, Confucius-ella," he joked and pulled her closer to him . . .

Kleigh was jerked back into reality when she felt a hand tap her on the shoulder. She turned around and saw the mayor standing behind her with a smile on her face. It took Kleigh a few seconds to gather herself because she could almost still smell the scent of Tron's cologne and feel his touch. She cleared her throat and returned the mayor's pleasant expression.

"Mayor Brown, you look lovely," she said, commenting on the baby-blue gown the mayor had opted for.

The mayor was an older black woman in her late forties. She wore her hair in a cute, short hairstyle, and she had a pretty face. She had the body of a woman who had been an athlete in her earlier days, which made her look good in the dress she was wearing.

"Thank you. You look quite stunning yourself," Mayor Brown responded.

"You're too kind. This event is just amazing. It looks like everyone is having a good time."

"That's because everyone is going overboard on the free champagne," Mayor Brown joked with a laugh. "Now, where is that brother of yours?"

"I'm not sure," Kleigh said glancing around. "I haven't seen him, but then again, I've been in and out of the kitchen since I got here."

"Always hands-on. I like that. I'm so glad I chose your bakery to do the desserts. Everyone has been raving over them. Especially those chocolate-covered strawberries and the red velvet cake! A few have even asked if you are available to cater their next events."

"Send them my way, and we can make it happen!"

"Perfect," Mayor Brown said.

A tall man came up to her, leaned down, and whispered something in her ear to make her giggle. She lightly tapped him on his arm and turned back to Kleigh.

"This is my husband," she explained. "Always a goof. But before I'm whisked away to the dance floor, please extend my apologies to Kevin."

"Apologies?"

"Yes. I saw that the theater he wanted to turn into a museum was blown up yesterday. You don't want to know the loads of paperwork that have been dropped on my desk in a measly twenty-four hours. So far, terroristic activity has been ruled out since no one was killed in the explosion, thankfully. A few federal agents have been sniffing their noses around, but I told them that I don't think Kevin had anything to do with it. After all, I was going to sign off on his ownership of the property next week. Whoever did this has a personal vendetta against your brother, so please tell him to watch his back. He's done a lot of good for this community. I would hate to see another young black soul lost," Mayor Brown said and squeezed Kleigh's hand. "But I said that tonight, I was going to enjoy myself and go back to work tomorrow. I'm so sick of the people in New York not knowing how to act. Explosives? Really? Have a good night, dear!"

The theater had gotten blown up? Kleigh stood there with her glass in hand, looking stupid. That was probably why he had gone overboard on the calls and texts the day before. He must have been genuinely worried over her whereabouts. Downing the rest of the champagne, she stepped to the side and pulled her phone out of the black shoulder clutch she had. She scanned the ballroom to see if she could find her brother in the crowds, but he was nowhere to be found. Where was he? She called his phone and listened to it ring before he answered.

"*Now* you want to call," he answered rudely.

"I'm sorry," she started. "I was just feeling a little overwhelmed yesterday. I needed to get away." Pause. "I heard about the theater." Pause. "Hello?"

"I'm here."

"Did you hear what I said?"

"Yeah, I did."

"And you aren't gon' say nothing?" Kleigh asked, feeling herself getting frustrated.

"For what? You don't give a fuck that I'm out here tryna build an even bigger legacy for our name. You're too worried about running the streets and having fun, girl. That shit's dead. Especially when everything you do directly affects me."

"Klax, I wasn't the one who asked to be the boss. You did!" Kleigh said glancing around to make sure nobody was listening to her conversation. "When Daddy said, don't let nothing happen to me, he didn't mean try to control my life. I'm sorry about the theater, but I'm not sorry for ducking you and the babysitters you always have watching me. It would be different if you had niggas watching me as I moved around on my own free will. But you got these niggas trying to tell me what I can and can't do because *you* said so. I'm not going for that anymore."

"I can feel that, and after all this fire goes out, you have my word that I ain't gon' be all on your neck like I have been."

"And when will that be? Neveruary?"

"Hopefully, everything goes well tonight."

"Tonight? Where are you anyways? I thought you'd be at the mayor's birthday celebration."

"Nah," Klax told her. "That's where I'm expected to be. I'd rather be incognito tonight."

"Is everything all right?"

"It will be after I handle this business."

"I don't like the way you're talking, brother. Are you good?"

"Yeah. And by the way, I got my niggas on you right now too. You look nice in that red dress. Mama musta picked that out. I'ma holler at you a little later, OK?"

"Klax!"

But it was too late. He'd already disconnected the call. She groaned to herself, hoping with all her might that her brother wasn't about to go and do something stupid. She had an uneasy feeling in the pit of her stomach. There was something about Klax's tone that seemed off. She couldn't put her finger on it, but she tried to push it to the back of her mind and send positive thoughts up into the universe to keep her brother safe.

Chapter 10

"The truth is rarely pure and never simple."
—Oscar Wilde

Klax

It was later in the evening when Klax found himself two hours away from his home and outside of a boxing gym. He checked the address in the email that Adonis had sent to make sure he was at the right place, and sure enough, he was. From the outside, it looked like a nice gym. Like whoever the owner was had put a lot of time and money into it. He sat outside waiting for a while, watching men, young and old, enter or leave. He was supposed to be at the mayor's dinner but had decided at the last minute not to go. Once he saw Adonis's email, there was no way that he was going to wait another second to take action. He also figured that at the dinner, he would be something similar to a sitting duck. Now that he had arrived, he realized he had no idea what he was going to say to Sunny. He just knew he had to tell him to call his son off, whatever the cost. Klax had been playing nice so far and hadn't shown his hand yet, although he wouldn't have a choice if things didn't go smoothly that night.

He removed the key from the ignition of his Range Rover and got out of the car. Dressed for the occasion, Klax was wearing a black hoodie, a pair of gray joggers, and a pair of black Nike Air Max sneakers. He sauntered into the gym and hung back while he looked around. There was a ring in the middle of the floor high off of the ground. Around it was all types of workout equipment and people using them. It wasn't hard for him to blend in as he skimmed the place for the person he was looking for. The only photo Adonis could find of Sunny was an older one, but hopefully, he hadn't aged too much.

"Keep that right arm up! You're leaving your face wide open!"

The loud, gruff voice came from the ring, and Klax rested his eyes there. A boy who couldn't be much older than 16 was in the ring sparring with an older gentleman. They both had on boxing gear, so Klax couldn't really make out their faces. He watched amused as the boy kept getting frustrated when his jabs didn't land on the intended target. He was hitting all air. However, the older guy was laying into him.

"You did better than last time, Jake," the man said to the boy when they finished. "But you still have a long way to go. Hit the showers. Your mom is going to be pulling up in a moment to get you."

"Thanks, Sunny," the boy said and stepped out of the ring.

KIax watched as Sunny too climbed out of the ring and headed over to a water bottle sitting on a nearby bench. He waited until he saw him head into what looked like a back office. Klax maneuvered through the gym, keeping his eyes on Sunny until he reached his destination. Not wanting to surprise him, Klax knocked on the open door.

"If your mom is here, tell her she doesn't need to worry about paying this month, Jake. I'ma go ahead and cover that tab for her," Sunny said with his back turned toward the door.

He was in the middle of rummaging through some papers when the door shut.

"That's nice of you, but I ain't Jake."

Not recognizing Klax's voice, Sunny spun around to face him. He sized up the newcomer by looking him down, then up. When finally he got to Klax's face, a look of recognition crossed over his eyes. He rushed and reached for a pistol underneath the desk. When he went to aim it, Klax disarmed him easily and tucked the gun in his own waist.

"I take that as you know who I am."

"You better have a damned good reason to bring your ass up in here, boy," Sunny said with a glare.

Klax invited himself to sit down in the chair on the client side of the desk and motioned Sunny to sit down as well. Sunny sneered at him and shot daggers with his eyes.

"You aren't welcome around these parts, and I'm going to give you five seconds to leave."

"You're causing problems for my business, so, nah, I can't do that. Sit down. Let's talk about the bulldog you've released into Harlem and my other places of business."

"I'm not doing anything," Sunny spat. "Now, you have four seconds."

"You can continue to count down all you want, but until you order that son of yours to stop making noise where I make my money, I ain't going nowhere. Feel me?"

"My son? My son isn't in Harlem."

"Is that right?" Klax said and pulled up the security footage from the night Tron showed up at Diamonds on his phone. "That ain't LaTron?"

Sunny took a quick glance at the phone when Klax held it up to his face. He looked genuinely shocked to see Tron sitting across from Klax in the VIP section. The sound wasn't on, but Sunny watched him move his lips like he was trying to read what he was saying.

"No need to strain your eyes. I can tell you exactly why he was there," Klax said, putting his phone away. "He came to pay me a visit at my club to tell me that he wants the throne, and I'm here to tell you that's not gon' happen. I'm here to stay. I don't give a fuck about no birthright shit. That doesn't apply to the streets. What happened back then was between you and my pops. That eye-for-an-eye shit ain't gon' fly with me. He done made a little sound in Harlem, I'll give him that. I'm sure you heard about the bombing of the theater. That was your son's doing. That was also the last straw. Because if I show my hand, I'm gon' make the little bodies he's dropped look like a few grains of salt. Call him off."

"I can't do that," Sunny said, looking Klax square in the eye.

"What you mean you—"

"I can't call him off because I never sent him in the first place," Sunny said, shaking his head.

"And I'm supposed to believe that?"

"I don't give a rat's ass what you believe, boy!" Sunny said shooting Klax another glare. He sighed and took a seat across from the young man. "I wouldn't send Tron to Harlem. Especially after seeing what your father did to it. Back when I was on top, I ran things the right way. Of course, drug money was what kept the lights on, but it was also what fed the children. Bought books for libraries. Provided shelter and counseling for women dealing with domestic violence. That list goes on. Something told me to get out while I still could and take my family with me. But your father never gave me that chance. I knew he was no good when he approached me about doing business, and the only thing I heard come out of his mouth was how much money we could make together. That's all he cared about. *Money*. To me, money was a given, and I was making enough of that by myself. Had he come to me with a plan on how we could be fruitful to our community on top of making money, I might have considered it. However, I could see the greed in his eyes. That same greed led to my downfall.

"After that, I didn't want anything to do with Harlem. I packed my son up and started a new life here. I tried my best to keep that boy out of the streets, but fate tempted him. The operation he started here was good, but I guess not good enough for him if he's in Harlem trying to take down your empire."

"*My* empire? Not *yours?*"

"No, it hasn't been mine for a very long time. I've made peace with the past, and it is something that I will never seek again." Sunny paused and stared at Klax for a few moments. "However, just because I don't get my hands dirty anymore doesn't mean I don't keep my nose in the streets. I know who you are Kevin Klax Turner. Who you *really* are, I mean."

"Enlighten me then, Old School."

"I know that you are ten times the hustler your daddy was. I knew that when I heard about the trade school you opened up for convicted felons. I also knew that you put up a façade that you're *just* a kingpin."

"Of course, I'm not *just* a kingpin. I'm a businessman too," Klax said with a smirk.

"You have jokes, I see, but you know what I mean. You have these people thinking that you just run Harlem. You've been hiding in plain sight for years."

"I don't know what you're talking about."

"Don't you? You, my dear boy, are the buyer, but to New York, you are the connect."

Klax felt his blood run cold at the words that came out of Sunny's mouth. He was not only stunned but confused at how the old man could know something that nobody, not even Adonis, knew. The silence coming from Klax was the only confirmation Sunny needed. Klax could not combat the truth, but he was left to wonder how Sunny had come up on that kind of information about him. He assumed it was because he was once the head honcho and probably still had the same contacts. Still, he was right. Klax was not *just* Harlem's kingpin. Thanks to a fateful trip to Mexico the year his father died, Klax had become the sea of life to every hustler in New York. Nobody knew who the connect was. They just knew when and where to pick up their new shipments. To save face, Klax had many different grades of cocaine circulating the state, because if all of the same were floating around, he wouldn't be able to keep his secret. He even set it up so that he would receive a shipment from himself, so no one would ever even think he had as much power as he truly did.

"My son doesn't know what he's getting himself into," Sunny said. "I will talk to him."

"Nah," Klax shook his head. "I came here to offer a solution, not just tell you about the problem. I can't right my father's wrongs, but I can say that shit had nothing to do with me or what I have going on. I know you're out of the game, but I can offer Tron a seat at the high table. He can't be the kingpin of Harlem, but he can be the man here. As you said, the little operation he has here is nice, but with my help, he can tighten up. Elevate. Be bigger than he ever imagined. I'll go into more detail when we all have a sit-down. Can you set that up?"

"I can."

"The sooner, the better."

"How does tomorrow night sound? Here in the gym?"

"That sounds good."

"But I have one requirement," Sunny added with a mischievous look in his eye.

"And that is?"

"You get out there in the ring with one of my boys."

"You serious?" Klax grinned.

"You want me to call this meeting, don't you?"

"A'ight," he shrugged. "I need to warn you, though, I have a mean right hook."

"Let's see if you can make it do what it do then," Sunny said as they both stood to their feet. "And, son?"

"What's up?"

"I know you don't think you're walking out of here with my gun, do you?"

Chapter 11

"The best view comes after the hardest climb."
—Anonymous

Sunny

The morning after Kameron Turner's son suddenly popped up, Sunny found himself sitting on the balcony of his three-bedroom apartment. He was wrapped tightly in his Ralph Lauren robe and had a steaming hot cup of tea on the bistro table beside him. Below were children playing on the nice playground, laughing and having what seemed like the time of their life. He'd grown so accustomed to his simple life that he had truly forgotten what it felt like to live lavishly. Or maybe it was that he just didn't miss it. He was at peace, watching life move around him. However, it had taken life and its many experiences to put him in that mind-set. He should have known that his son would have taken on some of his early knuckleheaded ways. After all, Tron would have gotten it honest.

Sunny had been so focused on building a new life so that the old one could be left in the past he hadn't thought for one second to ask his son how he felt inside. He wasn't the only one who witnessed the loss of two people they loved. Tron was right there too. Sunny thought that if he could create something else for Tron to cherish, then maybe, those losses wouldn't seem too much in vain, but he was wrong. Tron had lied to him to seek the revenge that Sunny didn't. He had to admit; he was not the one who trained his son on the streets. No, that had been Kyan. Kyan had taken Tron under his wing when he was 18 and showed him the ins, outs, and how not to grab the rope, but to tug it. However, no matter how great of a street general Kyan had been, and still was, neither era was a match for Klax Turner. Sunny thought back to the sit-down and remembered how the hairs on the back of his neck stood up. There was something about Klax's presence that spoke so loud and clear that Sunny had no choice but to respect it. What Klax didn't know was that after he'd disarmed Sunny, Sunny almost put the blade he had in the pocket of his sweats on his neck. But something had stopped him. He couldn't, because although Klax and Kameron shared the same blood, they didn't share the same look in their eyes. When Sunny looked, he saw no greed there. Instead, he saw the same look he used to see inside his own eyes when he looked in the mirror: determination. Sunny figured that if Klax wanted to kill him, he would have done so when he took the gun. He figured what harm could he do by listening to the boy.

After hearing about what had been taking place, Sunny came to one conclusion. Tron may have won a few battles, but that was only because Klax had refused to entertain the war . . . as of yet. If Klax fought back, Sunny feared he would lose his son, and Tron was the only thing he had left. And he couldn't have that. If Sunny hadn't learned anything since being out of the game, he had learned that harmony was always the better choice. How powerful could any one man be if he was afraid to get out of his own way? So, if calling a truce was the only way to stop the bloodshed, then, so be it. He didn't like that both

Kyan and Tron had lied to him about Tron's whereabouts, but that was a pea to a giant.

Knock! Knock!

"The guest of honor has finally arrived," Sunny said when he heard the knuckles on the glass before the balcony door slid open.

"I came as soon as you called," Kyan said and shook Sunny's hand. "You sitting out here in the cold?"

Kyan slid the door closed behind him and stood with his arms tightly crossed over his chest. He was wearing a red Balenciaga hoodie, black jeans, and a cap on his head. Although well in his forties, Kyan always held a look of youth about him and carried himself with the swagger of someone half his age. He had never had children of his own, which was shocking given the fact that he always kept a string of women chasing behind him.

"It helps to keep my mind sharp. Have a seat with me."

It was a request, not a question. Kyan, being his oldest friend in the world, could recognize the terseness in his voice. Although he did raise a brow, he sat down in the chair on the opposite side of the bistro table.

"What's good, G?" he asked.

"You might be able to tell me better than I can."

"I might be able to if you elaborate a little more," Kyan joked.

"Where's my son?" Sunny asked dryly.

"He's in Denver, enjoying himself like any other young man his age."

"I'm going to ask you again. Where is my son?"

Kyan sighed before clasping his hands together. "He's been moving around Harlem."

"And you knew about this?"

"I had an inkling, so I went to check it out to see what he was doing around those parts. He wants—"

"To be who I used to be," Sunny answered. "But he wants it for the wrong reasons."

"He wants what should have been his," Kyan countered. "He would have been ten times the hustler that we were."

"He already is that," Sunny told Kyan looking him square in the pupils. "He doesn't need to dig up the past to try to be that. The moment you found out what he was doing, you should have told me."

"You're right about that, and I apologize, Sunny. I thought I was being a good uncle to my neph, but I should have put my loyalty to you first. The young nigga has heart, though. It reminds me of us back in our prime. I just wanted to help him flourish, that's all."

"And I can respect that. However, gunning for Kameron Turner's son is not the move."

"Why? Because you're afraid what happened to you will happen to him?"

"No . . . because if he continues on this path, my son will become the new Kameron Turner. As ironic as this sounds, Kevin Klax Turner is the me of his era. As much as it pains me to say that, it's true. Everything that I had hoped to accomplish during my time on top, he has already done in such a short time. He is more than a kingpin; he is a king. And because of that, he must be protected."

"You're saying that as if you know him," Kyan pressed curiously.

"I know enough. You want to know why I didn't want my son to go into the dope game?"

"Because of what happened to his mother and sister."

"I can see why you think that, but you are incorrect. I didn't want him to because I saw something greater in him. It took me awhile to understand why God had punished me so, but I finally understood. I was ready to let it all go and enjoy a long life with my family. But you and I know that there is only one way in and one way out. There was an exception made for me, a painful one, but an exception, nonetheless. I wanted to lead my boy down a different path, but fate tempted him toward something else. And since this life is what he's choosing, he needs to learn that sometimes princes are meant to stay princes, and there is nothing wrong with that. There is still a throne. I need you to get my son home. Tonight. By eight o'clock."

"Why eight o'clock?"

"He'll see."

"And what if he doesn't want to come?"

"Remind him that he washes all of his money through my businesses," Sunny said flatly.

"Well, that'll do it," Kyan said with a grin. "I'll get on it. Is there anything else you want to tell me before I skate up out of here?"

Sunny looked at him and mulled briefly over telling his longtime friend about the meeting that night with Klax, but he thought better of it. Instead, he picked up his glass of tea and drank the rest of the hot liquid before he shook his head.

"Not right now, brother," he said. "But I do have a question for you."

"Speak."

"When are you going to let this street life die? You might look young, but the truth is that you're getting up there in age. We both are. Don't you think it's time for you to settle down and get married? Maybe even have some little bigheaded Kyans running around?"

"I'll settle down when the money slows up," Kyan said with a grin. "Not all of us can open up a gym and be content with that."

"Why not?"

"Man, Sunny, I'm not about to have this conversation with you right now. We both know what happened the last time you got to talking about getting out of the game," Kyan said and lifted his hand for a handshake.

"Yeah, yeah, whatever, brother," Sunny said and slapped hands with him. "You ain't going to be saying that when you look up ten years from now and can't look your legacy in the eyes."

"Well, holla at me ten years from now," Kyan said and stood up from his seat. "I'm gonna leave you to sit in this cold air by yourself. Let me go tell this boy he needs to hurry home 'cause he got an ass whooping coming."

Sunny grinned as Kyan left. When he was once again alone and lost in his thoughts, he began to look forward to new beginnings. Back when he was younger, a merger with Kameron Turner was not the right thing to do, but maybe together, their sons could do something that neither one of them could have. Anyone else in Sunny's position might have thought it crazy for him even to consider putting the two men in the same room together. Or even attempting to make a union with the blood that had spilled his, but it was what it was. New beginnings couldn't happen if one were always looking at what once was.

Chapter 12

*"If treachery is the reward of trust, will the man who
trusts come to harm?"*
—Mahatma Gandhi

Tron

"Mmmm," the soft sound of someone stirring in their sleep got Tron's attention.

He looked down at the long, sleek hair on the head resting on his chest and found himself kissing the top of it. Kleigh had found her way to his home after the mayor's birthday dinner, and he had been prepared to send her on her way, but when he opened the front door for her, he changed his mind. She looked beyond stunning, standing there wearing a red dress and holding an overnight bag. She told him that she wished she'd been on his arm that night instead of all alone. So, he made up for it by massaging her body from head to toe and listening to her tell him about her night until she fell asleep.

Now, there they were entangled in each other's arms as the sun came up. He could honestly admit that no other woman could say that he'd cuddled her, but he wanted Kleigh to feel at ease. He wrestled with his conscience to convince himself that was the only reason he didn't push her off him. In the fast life that he lived, women were good for one thing and one thing only: a quick fuck. Once that was over, he sent them on their way and got back to the money. He had never even played with the idea of having a lady, and that hadn't changed . . . really. Still, he found himself kissing her forehead in her sleep before he could stop himself.

"Kissing me in my sleep, huh?" she mumbled cutely with her eyes still closed. "I must make you feel some type of way."

"Maybe, Sleeping Beauty. That's a problem for you?"

"No, I like it. Because you make me feel some type of way too," she said, snuggling a little closer to him. "Ever since that first time we met, whenever I think of you, I feel like a ray of light is inside of me. There is something about you, Tron. And I don't want you to go away until I figure it out, OK?"

She finally opened her eyes and looked up at him. Even her bare, morning, sleepy face was beautiful.

"A'ight," Tron said although he knew he was lying.

He had been so busy trying to deal with and enjoy the present that he didn't once think about what it was going to do to her when she found out that he'd lied.

"Can I ask you a question?" she asked.

"You just did," he teased, and she pinched him. "Ouch, girl!"

"Well, that's what you get for being stupid when I'm tryna be serious."

"A'ight, man, what's the question?"

"You don't want to fuck me?"

"What?" Tron asked, tickled by the forwardness of her question.

"I mean, last night after I got out of the shower, I was naked," she said, looking into his eyes. "You massaged my entire body before I got dressed, and you didn't once try anything. Do you not find me attractive?"

"Have you seen yourself in the mirror? Who wouldn't find all of that attractive? You're beautiful—beyond it, Kleigh. Don't play with me."

"OK, well, if you feel like that . . . Why didn't you make love to me? I wanted you to," she said, and for a second, their eyes locked intensely. "So, why didn't you?"

"You're a virgin," Tron answered.

That was partly the truth. The entire truth was that he didn't want to take something so sacred from her when he would eventually be the one to break her heart. He didn't anticipate falling for her. He didn't even know where he was falling. All he knew was that he was dropping at 1,000 miles per hour wondering when he would land. The emotions she sent through his body were foreign to him, especially feeling them so soon. He'd heard of a thing called "love at first sight," but he thought it only existed in white romance movies.

"OK, and what does that have to do with anything?" Kleigh asked, propping her head up on her hand. "I'm falling for you, Tron; I can't help it. It's something that I want. My virginity is mine to give, and I want you to have it. So, it doesn't matter if it's today or tomorrow . . . You're gon' be deep inside of me sooner or later. So why not now, baby?"

The way she said "baby" made his manhood jump to attention. Her voice was so soft and sexy, and the way her fingertips lightly rubbed his chest did something to his breathing. He knew what she was doing, and he was trying his best to remain unmoved, but it was proving to be impossible.

"Don't do that," he said in a low voice.

"Do what? This?" Kleigh leaned in and took Tron's bottom lip in her mouth, sucking and running her tongue across it. "Or this?"

Her hand traveled down his torso and stopped at his groin. Then it found what it was looking for, and he didn't stop her when she slid it inside of his briefs. He heard her inhale a small sharp breath when she felt his size, and her eyes lowered sexily.

"Damn..."

"I don't want to hurt you," Tron whispered. "Stop, please."

But she didn't. Instead, she stroked him up and down with her soft palm, making him even harder in her hand.

"I can handle it, I promise," she assured him. "Just go easy at first."

"No, that's not what I mean," Tron told her. "Please stop."

"I don't want to. I want you to please your body with mine. You can have me in whatever way you want. I'm a big girl. I'll take it."

"Uh-uh," Tron shook his head and tried to keep the beast at bay for a little longer. "I can't."

"Please, daddy," she moaned and kissed him again. "Please. You're making me beg you to fuck me for real? Fuck me! Please, just fuck me. Fu—"

Tron couldn't hold back anymore. He snatched her hand from his boxers and pinned her down on the bed. They shared a heated kiss as he climbed on top of her and used his knees to spread her legs. As he kissed her, he pressed his thick manhood against her clit and ground down onto her. He let one of her wrists go so that his hand could slide down the side of her face and stop to grip her neck. He drew his head back and looked down at her for reassurance.

"Are you sure this is what you want?" he asked. "Because I can wait."

"Yes," she breathed and gently moved one of his locs from his face. "I'm giving myself to you, Tron, because you are the only man in this world ever to make me feel butterflies in my chest. Time is just a figment. A few moments can feel like forever, and forever can be a few seconds. So, yes, I'm sure."

Their lips found each other's again briefly before Tron's hunger for her body took over. He ripped the thin camisole she'd worn to sleep down the middle and licked his lips when her perky breasts bounced free from their cage. Her light brown nipples stared him in the eyes, begging him for moisture. He took one in his mouth and rolled the other between his fingertips, switching when he felt like it. She tasted so good but felt even better wriggling beneath him from the pleasure jolts going through her body.

"Tron," she moaned in a whisper. "That feels so good."

He wanted to take his time and enjoy every inch of her body, so he went as slowly as he could. He kissed her belly down to her boy shorts underwear underneath the covers. He kissed her plump lips through her panties and inhaled the sweet scent of her womanhood.

"Fuck," he heard himself muttering as he slid the panties off. "This pussy is phat as hell."

"Mmmm," she responded and tried to scoot up away from him.

"Uh-uh," Tron said, gripping her hips and tossing the covers back. When he looked up at her, he saw that she was covering her face with her arms. "Move them out the way. You can't be shy now."

The second he could see her beauty again, he dove in tongue first. Her shaved pussy tasted as sweet as it looked. He licked and sucked on her clit until she clawed at his arms, but still, he didn't stop. Using one of his fingers, he slid it in and out of her tight opening as he sucked.

"Tron!" she whimpered loudly. "I don't know what this feeling is. Troooon!"

She grabbed fistfuls of his locs in her hands and arched her back deeply. He felt her clit jump ferociously in his mouth, and her back arched deeply as he brought her to her first screaming orgasm. It lasted about twenty seconds before her body relaxed again. He kissed her inner thighs as her legs quivered and looked up at her face. She had released his hair and had commenced to rubbing her own upper body in between her soft pants. Her eyes found his, and there was a look of lust so powerful in them, Tron knew what time it was. He knew what she wanted, and he was ready to give it to her. It felt like all of his blood had rushed to his erection, and his dick was dying to dive into something wet and warm. Before removing his boxers, Tron grabbed a condom from his nightstand. After putting it on, he repositioned himself so that he was on top of Kleigh. She wrapped her arms around his neck and planted a sloppy kiss on his lips as he positioned his thick eight inches of hard meat at her opening.

"Mmmm," she moaned when he slid the tip up and down the crease of her southern lips, jumping whenever he hit her clit. "Oh, Tron."

"It's gon' hurt at first, but then it's gon' feel good, okay?" Tron told her in between kisses. "You gon' take it?"

"Yes," Kleigh said, and Tron felt her grip on his shoulders tighten.

He gripped her hips and kissed her jawbone up to her ear so that he could whisper sweet nothings to her as he fought against her tightness. She tensed up when the tip of his dick opened her hole, but she didn't push him away. In fact, she opened her legs wider to give him more leeway. Tron's breathing became shallow when he felt how tight and wet she was, and he couldn't help it; he forced his entrance. He wanted to take it slow, but the beast in him was too thirsty for her loving. Her screams filled his ear, but he soothed her by rubbing her gently with his hands, coaching her through the pain.

"Feel me," he said in her ear. "Ignore the pain. We're one, you and me."

It took about eight strokes before he felt her body relax under his, and instantly, her moans of pleasure followed. Tron's toes curled at the end of the bed because the bliss shooting through him was almost too much to bear.

"Kleigh," he whispered and shook his head as he kept deep diving into her ocean. "This pussy feels good as fuck wrapped around my dick. You hear me, shorty?"

In a quick motion, he pulled her to the edge of the bed so that he could stand up and watch her take his thick meat. He placed his hands behind her knees and forced her legs up and wide open.

"Look at me," he commanded as he slid back into her.

Her face twisted in a grimace before she bit her lip, but she did as she was told. So many thoughts went through his head as he watched himself go in and out of her. She was so thick, and her breasts bounced from the power of his thrusts. Tron wished he could stay inside of her love tunnel forever. The sound of her wetness was like music to his ears, and in the midst of it all, he would have forgotten his own name had it not been for her screaming it over and over. His thumb circled her clit, and he felt it begin to throb again as he brought her to a second orgasm.

Damn, why does she have to be so perfect? he thought to himself. *I'm gon' break her heart, and I don't want to. I don't know if I can give this pussy up. I don't think I'll be able to give it up. I want it forever. This is my pussy, and I'll kill a nigga if he—*

Tron felt her jerk under him, and he pulled out as he too climaxed. He snatched the condom off and shot his warm sticky nut over her flat stomach, throwing his head back with a shout. She shook violently on the bed, and her juices shot all over his legs.

"Aaaaah!" they shouted in unison until their sensations calmed down.

It was obvious that Kleigh had no energy to move, but that was OK. Tron scooped her up into his arms and carried her to the master bathroom. The tub was the size of a Jacuzzi, and he set her down softly inside of it. He used his head scarf to wrap her hair up so the water wouldn't get in it. Once each strand was secure, Tron ran them a hot bath and washed her up first and then himself. When he was done doing that, he got out and ran some fresh water just for her.

"Thank you," she told him weakly and rested her head on the side of the tub.

"No problem, baby girl," he said and rubbed her cheek with his thumb.

"Can we spend the day together?"

"I don't see why not."

"You are everything, Tron," Kleigh whispered and shut her eyes. "Now that you have a piece of me, I hope that you stay for a while."

To that, Tron had no words, and in a way, he was glad that he heard the doorbell buzz.

"Stay here. Let me go see who that is."

"I'm not going anywhere."

Tron fought the smile that wanted to come to his face and wrapped a white towel around his waist. He left her in the bathroom to see who had decided to visit him before noon. When he stepped out of his bedroom, he closed the door behind him for privacy. He walked down the long hallway, through his living room, stopping at the intercom next to the front door and pressed the button to talk.

"Who is it?"

"Your unc. Let me up!"

Tron recognized Kyan's voice and buzzed him in. He unlocked the front door and sat down at the dining room table. Kyan entered shortly after, and Tron took notice of the indifferent look on his face when he glanced up from the weed he'd started to roll.

"What's the word, Unc?" he asked with a grin.

"You're awfully cheery this morning. Did you do what you came to do?"

"I'm making progress," Tron told him.

"Progress or baby steps? I got people telling me that you've been running around with some girl. I thought you were supposed to be focused on your mission, not getting your dick wet, Neph."

"She ain't just some girl," Tron told him with a sly smile as he licked the blunt wrap. "She's Klax's sister."

"Oh, really?" Kyan raised his eyebrow as if he were impressed.

"Yeah, really, so keep your voice down 'cause she's in the back."

"Why is she here? You let her know where you lay your head at?"

"I'm just doing what I have to do to get close to the lion."

"Well, you're doing a fine job at that. I thought you'd have made more progress by now. I thought when I gave you that information about the building Klax was looking to buy, you'd do more than just blow it up."

"I did do more than just blow it up. I made him mad."

"And how do you know that?"

"Because the silence is deafening," Tron said with a malicious smirk. "This is just the beginning. And I have the most valuable piece to the puzzle in my tub right now."

"You knocked that down?"

"Chill out, man," Tron said, trying to hide his smile and light the blunt at the same time.

"Well, for your sake, I hope you did."

"For my sake?"

"Yeah. Sunny knows you're here and what you've been up to this whole time."

The smile on Tron's face vanished at Kyan's words.

"I thought you said you were gon' buy me some time— not tell him."

"I ain't say shit to him. I don't know how he knows, to tell you the truth. He just called me to the crib this morning and told me to tell you to get home tonight at eight."

"I can't do that. I'm getting closer."

"Closer to Klax or closer to his sister? Because from the looks of that dopey-ass smile on your face, she's more than a lick."

Tron made a noise with his mouth and ignored the words his uncle had just said. He puffed on the weed a few times before passing the blunt to his uncle. The fact that his father knew where he was but didn't come see him himself was making Tron even more curious by the second.

"Like I said, I can't do that," Tron repeated.

"You don't have a choice, boy," Kyan said, handing Tron back the blunt. "He said if you aren't at the gym tonight at that time, then he's pulling the plug on all of the money washing you do."

"He can't do that shit."

"He can't?" Kyan said with a raised brow. "Try him if you want to. I'm just the messenger."

"Baby!" Tron heard Kleigh yell from the back room. "Can we go get something to eat? I'm starving!"

"Yeah," Tron called back. "Give me a second."

"Go handle that, Neph," Kyan said, getting up from the table. "And make sure you're punctual tonight."

With that, Kyan was gone almost as fast as he had come. Tron put the blunt out because it didn't matter how much he puffed. His high was blown. He clenched his jaw before heading back to the bedroom to get dressed and thought of an excuse to tell Kleigh about why he couldn't spend the day with her as promised.

"Was on my grind, it was my time. I ain't think twice, I paid that price, and we did this, nigga. . ."

Nipsey Hussle's voice blessed the inside of Tron's Ferrari as he pulled up to the gym. The parking lot was empty except for his father's old-school, cocaine-white Cutlass and a Range Rover that he did not recognize. Curious, Tron got out of the car and shook his hair out of his face as he made his way to the entrance of the tall building. When he stepped inside, the first thing that hit him was a gust of cold air, as usual. Sunny made sure to keep his cool for the athletes, no matter how cold it was outside. In the distance, he saw his father sitting in the middle boxing ring facing him. He was dressed in his usual comfortable attire, a Ralph Lauren sweat suit and a pair of sneakers. He was not alone. A figure with his back toward Tron sat there wearing a Fendi jogging suit with the hood pulled over his head.

"What's going on, Pop?" Tron said, heading toward the ring.

"Glad to see you could join us, son," Sunny said, standing to his feet as Tron got closer. "But before you come any closer, I'm going to ask you to remove any guns you have on you and place them in that bucket right there."

There indeed was a black bucket on the ground right by the ring, and when Tron looked inside, he saw that there were already three guns in it. He didn't understand what was going on, and he shot his dad a confused look. Sunny had never made him disarm before, and curiosity made his eyes shift back to the person sitting with his back to him. Not knowing who was there made him wary to not be strapped.

"What's this, Pop?"

"Put your weapons in there," Sunny instructed again. "The two on your waist and the one on your ankle. Do it now before you come up here."

Tron's eyes went from his father and then again to the back of the hooded figure's head as he slowly removed his weapons. If it had been anyone else but his father asking something like that of him, he would have told them to eat a bullet. When he was completely disarmed, Sunny nodded his approval.

"Good," he said and waved for his son to come up. "Take a seat."

The only seat vacant was the one Sunny had just stood up from, and Tron sat in it so he could face the hooded person. When he did, he wished he hadn't. He jumped back up to his feet with a sneer the second he saw Klax Turner's unmoved face.

"The fuck?" he exclaimed, unable to hide his shock. "Pop, what the fuck is he doing here? You setting me up?"

"Watch your mouth, boy, and sit down," Sunny said. When Tron didn't do as he was told, Sunny raised his voice. "I said, sit!"

Tron had half a mind to jump out of the ring and grab his gun, but the hard stare Sunny was giving him made him think otherwise. He respected his father more than any man on earth. He had bounced back from what would have driven anybody else mad and had raised Tron in the process. Still, Tron couldn't help but feel betrayed by his old man. How had he let the son of the man who had murdered his wife and daughter into his establishment? More so, why was Klax still alive? Tron reluctantly fell back down in the chair and shook his head.

"Yo, Pop, you bugging. You do know who this nigga is, right?"

"I'm aware," Sunny answered. "Klax came to me about some of the things you've been doing and wanted to call a meeting."

"A meeting for what?"

"To tell you to chill the fuck out, nigga. Damn," Klax's deep baritone spoke up.

"Language! If the two of you can't be civilized, then there is no point."

"My bad," Klax said. "I'm here to tell you to chill out."

"And why would I do that?"

"Because I don't beef with little niggas. I annihilate them. You think you're starting a war, but really, it's just a hissy fit. I'll admit, you turned up a little bit on me, and that's the only reason I'm blessing you with the opportunity to dead this shit."

"You crazy if you think that's even an option," Tron said and spat on the ground by Klax's all-white Retro Jordan 1's.

"He always like this?" Klax asked Sunny with a chuckle.

"Just hear him out," Sunny urged Tron.

"Where is your loyalty, Pop? With me, or with him?"

"With myself," Sunny answered simply. "And that means I'm going to go with the most logical out of the two of you."

"And that's not me?"

"Hell no!" Sunny said, forgetting his language rule. "You know it's not you, Tron. None of this is you, especially if what I'm hearing about how you've been moving is true. That is *not* the son I raised. Answer me this, LaTron, why do you really want to knock Klax off of his throne?"

"Because of what his dad did to you. To us."

"If anything, that situation should have taught you that you don't take what you haven't earned. If what happened in the past didn't happen, do you really think I would have had you take my place just because you wanted to?" Sunny asked, standing over Tron with his arms crossed. "Have you taken a moment to think past that and ask yourself what you're really doing? Because to me, it looks like you're chasing after revenge that isn't yours to seek. We both dealt with the pain of the loss of your mother and sister, but I chose to move forward with my life. You have to make the decision now if you're going to do the same, or if you're going to go backward."

"I can't change the shit my dad did. I'ma just put that on the floor right now. I apologize for what happened to your mom and sister. I don't know what I would do if I were in your shoes," Klax said, looking Tron in the eyes. "All I've ever tried to do my whole life was be a better man than Kameron Turner ever was. I'm a son and brother first, a businessman second, and a beast last. Right now, you're at the second part of that. I'm here to offer a truce and you a seat at my table."

"And if I refuse?" Tron asked.

"Then you meet the beast," Klax said simply.

Tron sat silently for a moment, pondering over the offer at hand. He could feel both Sunny's and Klax's eyes on him, waiting for him to answer. Just looking at Klax sent fire through his chest that was almost inextinguishable. Almost. If it weren't for the fact that he felt himself falling for Kleigh, that fire would burn forever. However, he knew that if he continued on the road he was on, their love affair would always be forbidden. The thought of not being able to see where the road would take the two of them was almost too much to bear. Killing Klax would hurt Kleigh deeply, and before she had given herself to him, he still would have taken the shot. But things were different now. He had planned to question her more about Klax's operation and whereabouts that morning but stopped himself because he didn't want her to think that was the only reason why he wanted her, even though, originally, it was. That inward battle with himself caused such a confused uproar inside of him that he almost didn't know what he was doing anymore. He thought that Kleigh would be his key to take down Klax, but the more time he spent with her, he questioned even opening that door. As he sat there, so many emotions were surging through him, but in the end, he clenched his fists and let out a resentful breath.

"A'ight."

"A'ight?" Klax asked, almost sounding shocked.

"That's what I said, ain't it?"

"OK, then. Before we go any further, I need you to call your dogs off. That stunt at my sister's bakery was uncalled for. With the Feds sniffing around, none of this is good for business."

"Something happened at Kleigh's bakery?" Tron asked, sitting up straight in his chair. "I wouldn't have ordered a hit there. I know how much it means to h—"

"Yo, how would you know how much anything means to my sister? Or her name for that matter? You sound like you care—like you know her."

Tron suddenly realized that he had spoken too much. The look in Klax's eyes was indescribable, and he could have shot himself in the foot if he still had a gun on him. He tried to think of a way to clean up what he'd said but couldn't. The only thing to say was the truth . . . partly anyway.

"I met her at the club that night," Tron finally answered. "I was going out; she was going in. I ain't know who she was at the time."

"And when you found out, what? You were gon' use her to get to me?"

"Yeah," Tron said honestly. "I was. But then I got to know her, and shorty was cooler than ice. I fuck with her. Truthfully, she's the only reason I just said yes to your little truce."

"Nah. You said yes because you knew I was gon' make good on my promise to blow your head off your neck," Klax told him. "And now I might still do so if you hurt my sister."

"Nigga, ain't nobody gon' hurt Kleigh. I fuck with her, though," Tron repeated himself a little more forcefully than he intended to.

"Does she know who you are?"

"Nah."

Klax was silent for a moment, and it seemed as if even Sunny was holding his breath. His eyes went back and forth to the cold stares the two young men were giving each other. He inched forward so that he was almost in between them just in case they were about to decide to put the ring to use.

"Then I guess it would be best if we don't tell her about all this, huh?" Klax said with a straight face. "If you gon' rock with me, and you say you ain't have nothing to do with the bakery, then your first job is to find out who did. We can chat about how you ruined my museum plans another time."

Boom!

The gunshot came out of nowhere and struck Sunny in the side. He fell to the ground with a groan, clutching his wound with shock frozen on his face.

"Pop!" Tron shouted, jumping to his feet to try to rush to his father's side.

"Aht aht aht, don't do it. Let that stupid nigga bleed out," a voice that he knew all too well said.

Tron looked at the entrance of the gym and was shocked to see his uncle Kyan standing there, pointing a gun their way. His cold eyes were on Sunny who lay writhing on the ground as his blood dripped into the ring. Kyan looked disgustedly at what was thought to be his best friend as he got closer to them.

"Unc, what the fuck are you doing?" Tron shouted, but Kyan just laughed at his grief.

"What does it look like I'm doing, Neph? I'm crashing the party."

By that time, Klax too had stood up to face the newcomer. He was still as a board and spoke no words. His eyes never left the gun in Kyan's hand, even when the older man started talking again.

"Sunny, is this why you didn't tell me why you wanted Tron to come home? Because you were tryna form some kind of alliance between my operation and Harlem?"

"*Your* operation?" Tron asked.

"Yeah, boy, mine. Have you ever stopped to think about your position and who put you there? *I* introduced you to everyone you know. You wouldn't have shit if it weren't for me putting you on. Why do you think any of them niggas listen to you? Because of *you?* Nah. They listen to you because *I* tell them to," Kyan sneered and turned back to Sunny. "You always were soft, even back in the day, brother. Always wanting to keep the peace until you got out of the game. But any true hustler knows there is only one way in and no way out."

"W-why, Kyan?" Sunny asked through quick breaths.

"Why did I just shoot you? Easy. Unfinished business. You see, you remember when Kameron approached you about going into business together, and you turned his offer down? Well, he came to me next and put something else on the table. He told me that if I gave him what he wanted, then he would give me my own territory. I believed him. You never wondered how he figured out your address? I told him where you lived and when you would be most vulnerable. But when he didn't finish the job to boost his own ego, I knew I had made a mistake. The moment you were out of the picture, Kameron went back on his word."

"So you're telling me that my mom and sister are dead because of *you?*" Tron asked, clenching his fists so tightly that his nails dug into his chin. "*You're* the reason for all of this?"

"Save it, boy. Kameron wanted Sunny bad, and he was gon' get at him eventually. I just sped up the process. And when that failed, I started my own shit up here in Albany and molded you in my footsteps. I molded you in my image, Tron. I taught you everything you knew about the game. I even put my hunger to be number one in your brain."

"You're the one who told me about what happened to my father," Tron said as the reality hit him. "You always reminded me of the story because you wanted me to seek revenge one day."

"Bingo. See, you're a lot smarter than you look, you know that? Eventually, after all those talks we had, I saw the poisonous seed I'd planted in your head sprouting. The hatred for Kameron Turner and everyone connected to him ran deep in your veins. You even distanced yourself from your father because you felt that he wasn't a man for not retaliating. I knew that eventually, you would go after the person who had hurt your family, or the next best thing. His son. It was too perfect."

"And what would have happened if I would have succeeded in killing Kameron's son and taken over his territory?"

"You wouldn't have gotten that far," Kyan said with a grin. "You would have been put to a forever sleep before you even got to enjoy the benefits of your actions."

"Once a snake, always a snake, huh?"

"Never a snake. More like a lone wolf," Kyan said and aimed the gun at Tron's head. "This ain't easy, you know. I love you like a son. But living a lifetime of being second in command just isn't what I want for myself. I want the world . . . starting with Harlem."

"Well, you can't have it," Klax's voice sounded as he brandished a small .22 from the back of his waist.

Before Kyan could shoot Tron, Klax began letting his gun off in his direction. Kyan was forced to drive back, and Tron jumped out of the ring, going for his own guns. By the time he wrapped his hand around the butt of one of his pistols, Kyan had already run out of the building.

"Let him go," Klax told him when he started to go after Kyan.

Tron wanted to go after him, but Klax was right. Sunny needed him. Tron climbed back inside the ring and knelt by his father's side. Sweat covered Sunny's forehead, and his breathing was quick. When he saw his son next to him, he lifted a bloody hand, and Tron grasped it tightly in his own. He unzipped Sunny's jacket and lifted the bloodstained white T-shirt Sunny wore to get a better look at the wound and winced at the sight. It didn't look good, and blood was pouring from it like a stream.

"Here, put this on the wound," Klax said, removing his hoodie and handing it to Tron. "I'll call the paramedics."

Tron took the hoodie and pressed it firmly on the place where the bullet had entered his father's body. All he had to do was hold on until help arrived. Sunny looked at his son and gave him a sad smile with bloody teeth.

"Son," he tried to say, but Tron shook his head.

"If you're tryna tell me goodbye, save that, Pop. You'll be just fine," Tron told him, but the crack in his voice said otherwise.

"I don't think I'ma make it out of this one," Sunny told him weakly.

"Don't talk like that, Pop. Just hold on until the ambulance gets here."

"I've held on long enough," Sunny told him in between breaths. "I got to see you grow into a man, and I'm proud of you, LaTron. So proud. You've had me a lifetime. It's only fair that you share me with your mom and sister now."

"Pop, just hold on," Tron said as his eyesight got blurry and hot tears rolled down his face. "Just hold on, please." Flashbacks of when he was a little boy came to his mind. He remembered seeing his dad get shot in front of him and how he cradled his father's head until the ambulance arrived. He hadn't felt such a terror as that since then. But when Sunny survived a gunshot to the head, he just knew his father would be around forever. But forever was cashing in too soon, because there Tron was again, with that same terror in his chest.

"I love you, son. Don't you ever forget that," Sunny said. "I-I'm sorry if you ever felt that I thought you weren't good enough for following in my old footsteps. But r-really, I've always thought you were a better man than I am and was. That's why it's important for this alliance to happen. Everything I couldn't do or finish, you boys can. But promise me one thing."

"What, Pop?" Tron said, trying to hold back the sob in his throat.

"That if y-you ever have the serious thought about getting out of this life, do it that moment. Don't wait for o-one more drop. Because that o-one more d-drop will t-turn into a hundred m-more drops. You hear me? D-don't fall into that endless cycle like I did. D-don't be like Kyan. I l-love you."

"I love you too," Tron said.

Those were the last words Sunny heard before he smiled one more time at his son and closed his eyes. Tron watched his chest go up and down as he let out his last breath. He knew he was gone because he felt his hand grow limp in his, but he didn't let it go. He pulled his father's lifeless body to him and held him as tightly as he had when he was just a boy. His head bowed, and his locs hid his face as he cried silently. He had never before known such a strong feeling of loneliness . . . no . . . of emptiness. He continued to hug his father until the paramedics arrived, and even then, letting go of his body was the hardest thing Tron had ever done.

"What happened here?" a woman's voice asked.

"I don't know," Tron heard Klax tell her. "We just came to get a late-night session in, and we found his father like this."

When Tron stood up to his feet, the young white paramedic knelt by Sunny and attempted to find a pulse. Tron wanted to tell her there was no point, that he was gone, but he was too rocky. A hand on his shoulder helped him to steady himself. He turned around and saw that it was Klax standing beside him with a solemn expression.

"You want to get out of here?" he said in a low voice and handed Tron back all of his guns so no one would see. "I already grabbed all the security footage."

"Yeah," Tron nodded and glanced at his father's lifeless body one more time. "Yeah, let's go."

Before they could be asked any more questions, the two men left the gym. Kyan's face burned a hole in Tron's mind, and all he could think about was how he wanted to empty a clip into it. The true reason for his family's demise had been so close to them that whole time, and nobody knew it. One thing that Tron had always admired about Kyan was his patience to see things through. Now, knowing that one of those things was him made Tron feel a rage that there was no coming back from. Kyan had planted a seed inside of Tron so that he would self-destruct, and Tron had fallen right into the trap. He'd never forgive himself for playing Pinocchio. The only thing he could do was settle the score.

"Nah, you rolling with me," Klax said when Tron started to go to his vehicle. "You don't need to be behind the wheel right now."

"I'm good. I need to go back to my crib."

"Cool, I'll take you. Hop in before the police get here," Klax said, motioning his head toward the Range Rover Tron had seen when he'd pulled in. "It's only a matter of time before they show up. We got lucky in there with the paramedics, but you can bet the boys in blue will ask a million questions."

Klax headed toward his car without checking to see if Tron had listened. Tron had more than half a mind to disregard his words, but he knew they were true. He didn't know what he would do if he got behind the wheel of his car. He didn't even think he would be able to focus on the road with the millions of emotions coursing through him. A part of him wanted to go to the hospital with his father's body when they put him in the ambulance, but what would he do when he got there? His feet were moving toward the passenger side of the Range Rover before his mind even told them to. He got in, inhaled the Black Ice car freshener, and reclined the seat back.

"Where to?"

"New York City," Tron told him.

"New York City?" Klax asked as he backed out and tried to avoid hitting the ambulance parked at an awkward angle beside him. "That must be why we couldn't find you. You were hiding too close."

"The best way to do it," Tron said in a monotone voice.

"What you need to get from there?"

"I just need to make sure everything is everything. Kyan knew I was staying there."

"A'ight. I'ma take you there. Then you can crash at my crib until we dead that nigga."

Tron grew silent and tried not to focus on one thing for too long. He hadn't felt a loss like the one he'd just experienced in over twenty years. He had forgotten about the pain that came with it. His heart was heavier than it had ever been, and suddenly, everything that he'd done the last few weeks seemed pointless. He thought he was delivering his father's honor back, but Sunny had that all along. He walked away from what he felt wasn't good enough for him anymore. And there Tron was, trying to get it back like a fiend.

"Speak your thoughts," Klax told him after they were driving on the interstate for a while.

"I don't got none."

"Fair enough. Then I'll speak mine," Klax told him with his eyes on the road.

"You don't need to do that; I don't need your sympathy."

"And I didn't plan on giving you any. All I was gon' say is I know how it feels to watch a father die in front of you."

"You saw your pops die?"

"Yeah," Klax nodded. "I did. It wasn't nothing like what you just saw, but death is death. There was a time when I thought my old man was invincible. I never knew him to lose a fight, ever. I saw that nigga crack a man's skull with his bare hands before so to see a silent killer like cancer make him so frail and weak did something to me. I guess in a way I would have rather have seen him die from a bullet than to have watched him wither away into nothingness. He wasn't the best man, I can admit that, but that just helped me to see who I wanted to become. We choose our own paths and create our destinies. The last day I saw him alive, he'd asked to see me alone because he had something important to tell me."

"What did he say?"

"He told me that his death was going to give me the power to be better than he ever had been. That everything he had ever done had been so that when I was ready, I'd have more than one choice of who I could be. Then he gave me a plane ticket to Mexico and told me that when he was gone, go there to clear my mind. And when I was ready, come back."

"So what are you telling me? To go to Mexico?"

"No," Klax said in all seriousness. "I'm saying that before you dive back in, before we go after Kyan, you need to clear your head. Your father's death didn't come in vain. It came with the gift of knowledge. Now you know what you're dealing with, but before you can handle it, you need to be centered. Kyan knows you, and if what he said was true, you no longer have an army behind you. I can guarantee you that all of those niggas already have orders to dump into you on sight."

Tron knew that the words Klax spoke were the truth. Still, he couldn't even fathom sitting around and doing nothing when Sunny's death so fresh. He also didn't care about Kyan taking his army back. Tron would take them all on if he had to.

"I'm not about to hide from this nigga. So if that's what you're asking me to do, you can just save all that."

"Two devils battling will only create more fire. You can't beat the dark with more dark. The only thing that's been fueling you for this long is hate. Kyan instilled that in you. You gotta let that shit go. What did your father teach you?"

"To love and forgive," Tron answered.

"And that is how you beat out the dark."

Klax's words came full circle, and Tron didn't just hear them. . . . He felt them. He replayed them in his mind a few times before, surprisingly, he found himself chuckling.

"Who do you think you are, G? The Nipsey Hussle of New York?"

"Nah, RIP, my nigga, though," Klax said with a smirk. "I'm just saying I need everybody around me to move in sync with me. I don't jump just because a dog barks. I don't even jump when he bites."

"So, when do you?"

"Never. I let that dog wear himself down, and then I take him out. Kyan will expose his weak spot soon, just like you did."

"I ain't do shit. I had you shaking on your own turf," Tron told him.

"You think so?" Klax raised his eyebrow in amusement. "Or is that what you thought?"

"I *know* so. I don't have a weakness."

"You do. Your thirst for revenge and to be on top," Klax said simply.

"That's not a weakness. You're supposed to strive to be the best."

"The best at whatever it is you're good at. You wanted to be in my position so badly that I bet you didn't even stop to think about if it was the right fit for you. The problem with you niggas is that you want power because it's power. And that's it. You don't even put a single thought past that. For you, your hunger to get even fueled your thirst so much to the point where you couldn't even see that you were being manipulated. And that makes it a weakness. Kyan used that to his advantage, and now we have to make him pay for that."

"We?"

"Yeah, 'we.' With the job I have in store for you, I'm gon' need you sharp and with no baggage, feel me?"

"I feel you."

Tron directed Klax the rest of the way to his apartment complex. There were a few things that he needed to grab before he left the place behind. It wasn't good that Kyan knew exactly where to find him, and staying there would still make him a target. When finally they arrived, Tron told Klax to hang far back so that he could look out if he needed to. He got out and bounded toward the door, but he didn't even make it that far before he saw a slew of flashing lights speed into the complex's parking lot. Police sirens blared in his ears, and when he spun around, he saw that he was completely surrounded. There were about ten squad cars, and the police officers wasted no time in hopping out to aim their guns at him.

"LaTron Walker, put your hands up where I can see them," one of the police officers shouted. "Now!"

In the times they were in, Tron didn't know if he would even get the chance to raise his hands. He didn't know if the officers would open fire on him the moment he moved a muscle. He didn't have fear in him, but he was nervous. Not only because he hated the police, but he didn't know what they wanted.

"What's this about?" Tron asked, slowly raising his hands and squinting his eyes because the lights were blinding. "And why the fuck all y'all got your guns pointed at me?"

"Cuff him!" the officer shouted, ignoring Tron's question.

"Ain't nobody fucking touching me, yo. Not until you tell me what the fuck's going on."

"We received an anonymous tip that you had something to do with the bombing of the theater in the Bronx," the officer told him as others advanced on him with a pair of handcuffs. "When we got clearance on a search warrant to check this address, we found the same kind of explosives that were at the scene of the crime. You are being charged with arson by explosion and arson by possession of explosive devices. If you resist arrest, we have no problem bringing you in by using excessive force, boy!"

"I didn't blow up shit!" Tron said, which was partly the truth.

"The evidence in your home suggests otherwise," the officer said and held up a large black bag. "There are enough explosives in here to take down half a block. Not to mention the drug paraphernalia we removed from the residence."

"I don't know how that got in there, because it wasn't there when I left," Tron said, realizing that Kyan must have got there before he did and planted the explosives. Instead of taking his life, he was trying to do something much worse—take his freedom. "You're gon' try to stick me with a little weed too?"

"Anything to keep you lock—"

"Wait! That's my boyfriend!" a woman shouted running through the officers and up to Tron. "Please don't take him!"

She wore a long, forest-green petticoat and a black hat over her bushy hair. He recognized her as a woman he'd seen a few times coming and going from the apartment complex. She couldn't have been more than 21, and Tron didn't remember ever speaking a word to her in his life. Not even a hello. But there she was, throwing herself over him as if she'd known him for forever. She wrapped her arms around his waist and stood on her tiptoes, kissing him deeply.

"OK, enough of that," an officer said and pulled her away.

"I love you! You'll be home soon," she said to a confused Tron. "Use the number you know in the morning!"

And just like that, she was gone faster than she came. She must have been high off some strong drugs. One of the tall officers aggressively pulled his arms behind his back to handcuff him.

"Check him!"

Shit, Tron thought to himself remembering the weapons on him as the officers patted him down.

None of his weapons were registered. He had never in his life been caught slipping, and now the one time he did, it was in a major way. Tron felt the officer's hands pause on his waist, and he stopped breathing.

"He's clean!" the officer said, and Tron held up his poker face.

At first, he was shocked because he knew for a fact that he'd had his guns on him. He looked to see where the woman had gone. She went back to where Klax's vehicle was parked in the distance and was handing him something through the window. Tron realized then that she must have taken his weapons off of him when she'd embraced him.

"No matter. We have enough to send him away for a long time," a new voice said approaching Tron. He was a tall man with blond hair and frigid eyes that never left Tron. "My name is Detective Hanes, and it looks to me like you've gotten yourself in quite a pickle here. Do you care to explain how and why you've been here less than a month, yet have managed to do something so fucking stupid?"

"I just told you, I ain't do shit."

"Maybe you didn't, but somebody did. Maybe you were just holding on to the rest of those explosives for somebody else. Somebody like Kevin Turner."

"I don't know who you're talking about," Tron told him, not batting an eye.

"We know he had something to do with this. It's just like someone of his . . . kind . . . to send someone like you to do his bidding."

"His *kind?*" Tron scoffed.

"Yeah, people who don't want to get their hands dirty, so they have those who are lower on the food chain do it. As I said before, I know Kevin played a part somewhere in this story. The bombing was too calculated; too direct. So if you tell me what I need to hear, I can assure you that you will be granted clemency. Did Kevin Turner assist you in any way with the bombing of the Old Royal Theater?"

"I just told you, I ain't do shit to no theater," Tron answered, raising his lip.

"Hmm," Detective Hanes smirked. "I hope you keep that same attitude in jail. I'm going to see to it that you don't get bail."

"Ain't this the point where somebody is supposed to read me my rights? Get the fuck out of my face, man."

"All right," Detective Hanes said.

The detective faked like he was about to turn around to walk away, but instead, punched Tron hard in the gut. As he went to double over from the blow, Detective Hanes followed the gut punch with a blow to Tron's jaw. Tron groaned and spat a big glob of blood to the concrete on the ground.

"You're lucky I'm in these cuffs," Tron said trying to eat the pain shooting through his body. "You'll see me for that."

"Add threatening a detective to his charges," Detective Hanes said as he headed back to his squad car. "Take him in."

The officers near him forced Tron to stand up straight before tugging him to a squad car. They forced his head down and pushed him inside the uncomfortable back-seat of the vehicle before shutting the door and getting in themselves. As they drove away, they passed the Range Rover, and although the windows were tinted, Tron was certain that he and Klax were holding the same solemn expression.

Chapter 13

"You change your life by changing your heart."

—Max Lucado

Klax

After watching Tron get bumped up, the answer to Klax's problem had finally come. He figured that by paying the woman passing his car several hundred dollars to remove all of Tron's guns from off of him, he had done his good deed. No truce would have to be carried out, and all Klax had to do was rid the world of Kyan for everything to go back to normal. What had taken place might have been Tron's Karma coming back to bite him, or maybe fate was tempting another hand. However, something about it all still didn't feel right. Although he was used to the fast life, the past few weeks had gone too quickly for Klax. Just a few days ago, he wanted to kill Tron in his tracks, but not so much anymore . . . which was how he ended up at his sister's place the next morning.

"Uh-uh, you can't come up in here and not explain why you weren't at the bakery's biggest event," Kleigh said when she opened the front door. It was early morning, and she was in a silk leopard print pants pajama set with a red silk robe. She blocked the entrance and put a hand on her hip. "*And* I didn't hear from you at all yesterday! You had me worried sick!"

"My bad," Klax said, putting his nose in the air to smell the aroma coming from her home. "You cooked?"

"Nope."

"Girl, I smell that bacon. Open this door," he told her with a grin.

She smacked her lips and added an eye roll for effect before she allowed him entrance. The smell was even more pleasant inside, and knowing her, the food tasted even better. He had to admit, Kleigh was gifted in a kitchen. She could make anything taste delicious, even if it was just a grilled cheese sandwich. He went to the kitchen and was about to grab a piece of bacon, but she smacked his hand.

"Boy, you better wash your hands! You might have been with some nappy-headed hoochie last night."

"The only nappy-headed hoochie in my life is you," Klax said, eyeing her bed head. "You probably got a few birds in that shit."

"See! Nope, get out!" Kleigh said, pretending to be offended. "I can be ugly in my house in peace if I want."

"I ain't going nowhere until you tell me how the mayor's event went," Klax said and obediently washed his hands in her kitchen sink.

She handed him two napkins. One to dry his hands, and one so that he could wipe his hands while he was eating. She pointed to the table and commenced to filling his plate with eggs, bacon, and her homemade French toast.

"It was probably one of the most amazing experiences of my life. Everybody loved the desserts, like, *loved* them. We even booked a few more upcoming events, so I'd say that it was a success. I wouldn't have to tell you how it went if you were there," she told him. "*You're* the one who plugged me with the mayor in the first place. I would have thought you'd want to see firsthand that I didn't do anything to jeopardize your shit."

"That could never happen. You're the best," Klax said, bowing his head to say his grace.

His eyes were closed, so he didn't see the fond smile she gave him. Kleigh made her plate and sat down across from him before saying her own grace and taking a big bite of her food.

"Oh!" she said and hurried to chew. "You haven't been answering any of your phones, but while I was there, the mayor told me something."

"What?"

"She said that you might be a suspect for the explosion. Apparently, some detectives have been coming around."

"Yeah, I know about that already," Klax said, thinking back to the night before and what he heard.

"They already questioned you?"

"Not exactly."

Before Kleigh could get another question in, a phone began to ring. By the girlish ringtone, Klax knew that it wasn't his phone. It was hers. He lifted his head and watched her grab it from her pocket and look at the screen. She made a face.

"Who is it?" he asked.

"I don't know. It looks like a jail number," she told him. "And I don't know anybody locked up, so it must be the wrong numb—"

Klax took the phone from her hand before she was done talking. Truth be told, he hadn't just gone over to her house because she made a mean breakfast meal, nor was it just to check on her. The woman he'd sent to remove all of Tron's guns was also supposed to pass on a message to call Kleigh's phone in the morning. When he looked down and saw that it was indeed a jail call, Klax figured either Tron understood the message, or he was going to call Kleigh anyway. Klax answered and went through all of the prompts to take the call.

"Hello?" he heard Tron come through on the other hand.

"I see you got my message," Klax spoke.

"It took me a minute; I can't even front. Shorty threw me for a loop. Good looking out on all that, though. You ain't have to do it."

"I know," Klax told him. "If it were me in your shoes, I hope you would have done the same thing."

"That's how I roll. Get down, lie down. On God, nem."

"Word. But what's good with it? How are they treating you in there?" Klax asked, ignoring Kleigh, who was mouthing, "Who is that?"

"Ain't shit good," Tron told him. "They said they're gon' hold me in this bitch without bond until my first court date. And that's a whole thirty days away. I'm gon' miss my dad's funeral."

"Don't even sweat that shit, G," Klax tried to assure him.

"Unless you gon' work a miracle for a nigga, I'm speaking facts," Tron said. "Just do me a favor. Handle all that for me."

"I can't even do that for you," Klax told him.

"I figured you'd change your mind about all this shit since I'm in here now. It's cool; don't even worry about it. I'm thinking this is where I belong anyway. I fucked up too bad."

"Nah, don't speak like that. Everything is still everything this way. I only said I can't do it because that's your ride to catch. I can carpool, but I ain't driving by myself. Like I said, don't worry about shit while you're in there. I have the best lawyer in the city."

"Yeah, well, he gotta be a miracle worker to get me out of this shit."

"You just keep your head up in there and let me do the rest."

"Why you wanna help me, man?"

"I don't know," Klax said, staring into his sister's eyes. "But now, it looks like we have the same problem. I'm gonna go 'head and get off this phone. I think somebody else might want to hear from you. You got a pen and some paper? Take my number down."

He gave Tron his main cell phone number before handing the phone to his sister. Kleigh was skeptical about taking the phone at first, but he insisted. She finally took it and placed it to her ear.

"H-hello?" Pause. "Tron? What are you doing in jail? Is that why I haven't heard from you? And how do you know my brother?"

Klax finished his food in the time it took Tron to answer her questions. Just in case she was furious when she disconnected the phone, he at least wanted to get kicked out on a full stomach. He watched a few tears fall from her eyes as she talked to him and heard the crack in her voice when she asked him what his charges were.

"Arson? T-they think you had something to do with the explosion? Well, you shouldn't have anything to worry about because you didn't do it." Pause. "Right?" Pause. "Tron?"

Suddenly, she withdrew the phone from her ear and just looked at it as if it were a foreign object. Klax went to reach for it, but her eyes jerked up, and she glared at him. Before he knew it, he had to duck quickly because she had launched the device at his head. It missed him by a couple of centimeters and went flying into the living room behind him.

"What the fuck is going on, Klax?" she demanded.

"Damn, Kleigh! You almost hit me!" he exclaimed.

"What the fuck is going on?"

"What did he tell you?"

"The phone disconnected before he could give me a yes or no answer about the explosion. *Or* tell me how he knows you. When we went out, he said verbatim to me that he doesn't know you. Did he . . . Did he do it? But why would he do that if y'all know each other? Wait!" Her eyes widened as if something had just dawned on her. "Is he one of your goons, Klax? Did you have him looking after me? He is, isn't he?"

"N-yes," Klax lied, relieved that she had given him an out.

"Really?" Kleigh asked and seemed genuinely hurt. "So, all this was just fake? He didn't even really like me? He was just following orders?"

"Well," Klax said, contemplating on letting her hate Tron. He still wasn't too fond of him running around with her or his plan to use her to get to him, but things weren't the same anymore. "He was supposed to watch you. So if he did anything extra besides that, knowing the risk of me killing him for it, I'm guessing it was because he liked you."

"Really?" Kleigh asked, blinking away the tears in her eyes.

"Really," Klax told her, reaching over the table to wipe the corner of her eye. "Now, dry your eyes. You're too pretty to look so ugly when you cry."

"OK," she said, smiling at his last sentence.

"My bad, sis. You know me, overly protective big brother Klax in the flesh. But to answer your question, no, he didn't do that shit. But I have it handled. I don't want you to worry your pretty head with my affairs. For the next few days, you'll notice heightened security measures, so I don't need you sneaking around, you hear me, Kleigh? Shit's getting real right now, and the streets are hot. Until I can cool 'em off again, I need to know that you're straight, a'ight? I want you to stay with Mama for a while. And you'll have to close the bakery until further notice."

"Close the bakery? You *do* know that you just said not to worry, but then gave me a lot of reasons to worry. What's really going on, Klax? Looking in your face, I can tell something has you on edge. Talk to me."

"Somebody wants a piece of what I have, and to get it, ain't no telling what they'll do. So, just in case, I'm taking all precautions. Just know I got it handled; trust me. Now, get dressed and pack a few things. I can drop you off on the way to my crib."

"I don't want to go stay with Mama," Kleigh told him. "I'll be fine here at home. Just have Drop or whoever else stand watch."

"I don't know, Kleigh."

"Well, what's the difference of me being there or me being here? I don't really want to be cooped up in that house with her. You know when she gets to talking, she doesn't stop. I want some kind of peace."

"Fair enough, but if that's the case, I'ma have somebody outside your door too."

"Fine."

"Don't be in here wilding."

"My nigga is in jail. There ain't much I can really do."

Klax opened his mouth, but then quickly shut it, making a disgusted face. Kleigh laughed at his expression and shrugged her shoulders. Suddenly, Klax's face grew serious, and he raised a brow at her.

"You're still a virgin, right?"

"Get out!" she shouted and pointed at the door. "Bye! Call me when I can get some of my freedom back. And make sure all of my employees get compensated for this shit."

Chapter 14

"You and I will always be unfinished business."
—Anonymous

Adonis

"Deeper! Please, baby, go deeper!" Bahli shouted into the fabric of Adonis's pillows. She was bent over, and Adonis was behind her digging her out doggie style. He was in heaven watching himself slip and slide all in her sticky goodness, but it was too good. So good that he wanted it to last awhile. He knew if he went too hard, then that would be all she wrote.

"I don't want to hurt you," he warned.

"I can take it," she pleaded.

"Let me enjoy this pussy," he told her, still stroking her at his own pace, and she smacked her lips.

"I'll do it myself then," she said, tossing her long weave over her shoulder to look back at him.

There was a devious look in her eyes right before she gripped the soft bed under her for support and began throwing her pussy back on him viciously. Her walls tightly gripped his shaft, and he felt his eyes begin to roll in the back of his head.

"Yeah, this pussy is good as fuck, I know," Bahli taunted. "This the best shit you ever had, huh?"

"Hell yeah," Adonis moaned and grabbed fistfuls of her thickness. "Shit, Bahli, you 'bout to make a nigga come."

"It's OK, baby, I am too. Oh shit!"

Adonis gripped her slim waist and began to match her thrust for thrust. Spitting on his thumb, he shoved it deep into her butt hole even though he knew she didn't like that too much. He didn't care. He was beyond turned on at that point. Bahli was a freak who rarely told him no. He felt her begin to quiver until she had no more energy to match his strokes, but that was okay. He could handle the rest.

"Adonis! Adonis! Adonis!" she shouted his name over and over.

The clear juices coming from her love tunnel turned into a thick cream as she came all over his dick. That did it for him. He couldn't hold back any longer. He shoved himself as deep into her as he could and came so hard into his condom that his toes curled. His entire body was rigid for a few moments until the overwhelming sensation passed, and then he collapsed on the bed beside her. Both of them needed a minute to collect their breath, but when she did, Bahli snuggled up to him.

"You always tryna make love to me," she teased, running a finger across his chest. "I am not your soon-to-be wife. I be needing to get fucked sometimes."

"I see," Adonis said and kissed her forehead. "And I don't have a soon-to-be wife anymore. I called it off."

"Really? You kicked Becky to the curb? I'm surprised."

"And why is that?"

"I don't know. It just seemed like she had you wrapped around her finger."

"If that's the case, how did you come into the picture?"

Bahli smacked her lips. "Don't play with me. I don't know one man with a loyal dick. But that woman had you jumping through hoops for a while. You reminded me more of a Tom than an Adonis."

"But you still always ended up in my bed."

"Because that dick is a Tyrone," she said, and they both laughed.

"Yo, you're wilding," he told her. "But, nah, you're right, though. I don't know who I was fooling with that one. I guess I was just tryna look at the bigger picture."

"And what was that?"

"Money. Power. You know, typical nigga shit."

"I hate you," she said and giggled. "You already have those things, with or without Miss Thing's money and connections. How did she take it when you ended it?"

"Bad. I saw her for who she really was," Adonis told her. "Her lawyer sent a letter to the office talking about she wants me to compensate her for all the money she spent on me during the time we were together."

"What are you gonna do?"

"I wrote the check," Adonis said. "Fuck that bitch. I don't need anybody for shit, and I damn sure ain't gon' let anyone hold things over my head. Her being out of my life helped me realize that she didn't fit in the first place."

"Good for you," Bahli said and leaned up to kiss his chin, but he moved, so her lips landed on his.

She smiled big, showing off her braces. He didn't know what she was thinking, but if it was anything deeper than what they had touched on the surface, she didn't let on. He was glad for it. After finding out that he was a single man, most women would have posed the question, "So, what's next for us?" But Bahli was the type just to let everything flow naturally. Right then, just lying together cuddled up felt good. There was no need to taint a good moment with complicated conversation.

She grew quiet after a while, and when Adonis glanced down, he knew why. She'd fallen fast asleep. Adonis too felt his eyes growing heavy, but the moment he decided to close them, someone knocked at the front door. He hoped that it wasn't Jessica's crazy ass because he didn't have the energy to deal with her. He got up from the bed, careful not to wake Bahli, and put his boxers on and headed to see who was there. He peered through the peephole when he got to the door.

"You ain't never heard of calling before you just pop up?" he asked, swinging the door open for Klax.

"Nah, not really," Klax said, walking in the condo but not too far inside. "You got a bitch here or something?"

"Or something," Adonis said with a grin.

"Well, this won't take long. I need a favor."

"What's good, boss?"

"I need your help to get someone out of jail," Klax said.

"No problem, who?"

"LaTron Walker," Klax said, and Adonis looked at him like he was crazy.

"Yo, ain't that the nigga who was hitting up your spots?"

"Yeah."

"And ain't he the one who fucked up your museum plans?"

"Yeah, that's how he got caught up."

"OK. Then why the fuck would you want to get him out?"

"It's complicated, but you gotta trust me on this one. He's with us now. I have a bigger problem on my hands."

Adonis sighed and shook his head. There were some things about Klax that he just would never understand, that being one of them. He didn't know what kind of game his friend was playing, but Klax had never steered anyone wrong.

"A'ight, man," Adonis said. "I'm assuming if they locked him up because of that, then they had some pretty hard evidence. How'd they get him?"

"They found explosives in his home."

"His dumb ass left the explosives in his home?"

"I don't think he would be that dumb. I think they were planted."

"By whom?"

"That's what I need you to find out," Klax said, handing Adonis a small piece of paper. "That's the address."

"You want me to go here?"

"Why not? It's been a minute since you were hands-on in the field."

"Because you always told me that you didn't need me."

"Well, now, I do," Klax said, looking seriously at him. "I need you to come through on this."

"Don't I always?" Adonis said glancing down at the New York City address. He sighed. "A'ight. I'ma get on it."

"Bet. I'm gonna head home for a few. Hit me when you have something," Klax said. "And, Don?"

"What's good, G?"

"Don't you think fucking my sister's best friend is cutting it a little close to home?"

"How—"

"She's the only one in the city with a lime-green Camaro. The same Camaro that's parked beside your car outside," Klax told him. "What happened to Becky?"

"That shit is dead," Adonis said. "After she let those feds in here, that was the last straw for me."

"Yeah, Bahli would look better on your arm. But if you hurt her, I hope you know how Kleigh is coming."

"Your crazy-ass sister, man," Adonis said with a grin. He held the piece of paper that Klax had given him up in the air. "But I'm about to see what I can do for your boy. I hope you're right about him."

"He was just misguided, that's all. Not all of us have the innate ability to want more instead of the same for ourselves. Sometimes, we all need a little bit of help to see a picture as a whole. We have bigger fish to fry."

"You care to tell me more about what's going on?"

"Right now, the less anyone knows, the better. Just do what you can for Tron as his legal counsel. Go as hard for him as you would for me. It's important."

"You're the boss," Adonis said and lifted a hand for a shake, but Klax just looked at it. Adonis grinned sheepishly. "Yeah, I might need to wash these."

Klax shook his head with a small smirk before leaving the condo. When he was gone, Adonis kept his word. He went straight for the shower so that he could head over to New York City that morning. It was still early enough for him to do what he had to do and still have time to come back home and enjoy Bahli's company for the rest of the day. Rest of the day? He didn't know what was coming over him. He felt as if she must have put that thing on him good if she had him wanting to get his business done and come back to her. When he was back in the room, he leaned down to kiss her on the cheek.

"I'm about to make a run real quick," he said when her sleepy eyes opened.

"OK, that's fine," she said and went to sit up. "I'll get dressed and leave when you leave."

"Nah, you're good; get some rest," he told her. "When I get back, I'll take you to grab some food. Maybe we can catch a movie or something."

"Really?" she asked with a happy smile.

"Yeah," he told her and stroked her hair. "I might be a little minute, so in the meantime, make yourself comfortable. Not *too* comfortable, though."

"You're so stupid," she said, lying back down. "I'll probably still be asleep by the time you get back. You really wore me out this time."

"Nah, that was you," Adonis said, going toward his bathroom.

His mind traveled to the place Klax wanted him to go. He didn't know what he was supposed to be looking for when he got there, and if he didn't find anything at all, he would have to figure out his next course of action. Either way, he couldn't let Klax down. There was something about his friend's presence that seemed off. There was a look of worry on Klax's face that Adonis hadn't seen in years, and it didn't sit right with him.

Chapter 15

"In any given moment we have two options. To step forward into growth, or to step back into safety."
—Abraham Maslow

Klax

When Klax got home, the hairs on the back of his neck stood up. He couldn't describe the feeling, but after he looked up and down his neighborhood, he dismissed it. He pulled his car around the circular driveway and took notice that his housekeeper, Tallon's, Toyota Camry wasn't posted in its usual spot in front of the home. She might have gone to the grocery store since she was the one who handled all of the house's affairs while he was gone. He didn't think too much about it since he was going to be in and out anyways. He was just coming to switch cars to something more low-key so that he could move around with ease. He stepped out of the vehicle and put his brown Tims to work as he made his way toward the home. The wind nipped at his ears, so he threw the furry hood of his Prada coat over his head and tucked his hands in his pockets until he reached the door. He unlocked it, twisted the doorknob, pushed it open—

Boom!

The explosion of his three-story home sent him forcefully flying back in the air ten feet onto the pavement.

The back of his head hit the concrete hard, but not hard enough to knock him out. Klax felt pain coursing through his body and heard a loud ringing in his ears. He groaned and tried to move, but his muscles betrayed him. Through extremely blurred vision, he saw black figures running toward him and thought his neighbors had come to see about him. He couldn't make out the words they were saying, but the closer they got, he realized that they weren't his neighbors. The automatic weapons in their hands were a dead giveaway. He tried to reach for his gun, but his motor skills failed him. The ringing subsided a bit, and when they got up on him, he finally could understand them.

"I'm about to air this nigga out right here," a gruff voice said.

"Kill him, and that's your own life. We're supposed to bring him in alive. Knock his ass out, though."

Klax was laid out on his back, staring up into the sun when a figure suddenly blocked his view. The next thing he knew, a man wearing Tims stomped him hard in the face, and then there was nothing but darkness. He didn't know how long he was out, but a splash of coldness brought him back to reality after what felt like seconds. He coughed and choked on what he realized was water after a few moments. He blinked his eyes feverishly until his vision focused, and he whipped his head around to get a better look at his surroundings.

No longer outside of his home, Klax was in a large, partially lit room that smelled badly of mildew. It was hot, and the air around him was very humid. The walls of the room were cement, same as the floor, and just a few lightbulbs were on the ceiling, making the lighting dim. He tried to stand up, but when he found he couldn't, he looked down at his arms and legs. His ankles, wrists, and torso were bound to a wooden chair, making it impossible for him to move. He was no longer wearing his coat or any shirt, for that matter. He was only in a pair of jeans and his Tims. Suddenly, his memory about the explosion and getting knocked out came back to him, and his heart pounded, not out of fear—out of anger. He summoned all of his strength and fought against his bindings, but it was no use. He could not get free.

"It's quite a feeling, isn't it? Feeling helpless, I mean," a voice from behind him said.

He didn't need to see the face to know whom it belonged to. He may have only heard it once, but that was all he needed for it to be etched in his head for eternity. Kyan stepped in front of him wearing a black True Religion sweat suit holding an empty bucket. He stood over Klax like a tiger overlooking his prey. The victorious expression on his face was enough to send fire through Klax's chest. He almost wanted to laugh. He had been worried about everybody else's safety but his own—the irony.

"Sorry about your crib, man," Kyan told him with a nonchalant shrug. "We had some extra explosives after planting the others in Tron's house. I'm sure you understand."

"So first, Tron, and then me," Klax finally said. "That's the game you're playing?"

"Does it look like I'm playing, boy? I mean, this whole shindig was entertaining; I can't lie about that. Especially seeing that nephew of mine run around doing all of the hard work for me."

"You might as well take the 'neph' out and just call him by his name. You betrayed him and killed his father in front of him. It doesn't matter what you do to me. You've already signed your death warrant."

"Who's going to kill me? Tron? Maybe you haven't heard yet, but he's going to be gone for a very long time."

"Is that right?"

"That's right. And your family's bakery would have been on his long list of charges had you not killed my men. I was going to take that building down too, but I admit I underestimated you. Which was why I knew I couldn't half step it the next time."

"So it was you that sent those niggas to my sister's bakery," Klax said finally believing 100 percent that it wasn't Tron.

"Guilty," Kyan said with a shrug. "I also knew he wasn't going to have the willpower to break her heart by killing you, so it was time to take matters into my own hands."

"Why am I here? I'm assuming you ain't do all that and keep me alive just to tell me sorry."

"Straight to the business, then, huh? A'ight, then," Kyan said and placed the bucket on the ground.

He grabbed another wooden chair from a corner and dragged it in front of Klax. He sat down and leaned forward, clasping his hands together. Klax thought he was going to start talking, but he stayed quiet and curiously stared Klax in the eyes.

"You gon' tell me why I'm here now or later? I got all night."

"You're a comedian too, I see," Kyan said with a grin.

"Nah, I only see one clown here. And that's you."

"I wouldn't be so quick to name call since you're at the mercy of this clown-ass nigga," Kyan said and pulled a joint from behind his ear before sparking it with a lighter he dug out of his pocket. He took a long drag and blew the smoke in Klax's face. "You're here because you have something I want."

"And what is it that you want? Harlem?"

"Bingo," Kyan said puffing on the joint again. "I want you to willingly step down from the throne and give me all of your territory."

"And why didn't you just kill me and take it instead of doing all this? Aah, yeah, I forgot, clowns love theatrics."

"Now you should know better than that," Kyan said. "If it were as easy as just killing you, you'd be burning right along with all of your property right now. Nah, I need you to let the streets know that I'm the NIC now. The clout you have is spread long and wide. Everyone speaks so highly of you, even your competition. So if I just take over, no one will listen to me, and there will be nothing but chaos. You know that."

"And you think they'll listen to me if I tell them that you got the juice now?"

"I know they will. These people, they think you're their king."

"Nah, they just look out because I do. That's the problem with niggas like you. Everything is about control and power to you. So what makes you think that I would even consider some shit like that? You might as well have killed me. Because that ain't gon' happen. Not even if hell froze over."

"Not even if I have something that you want?"

"You don't have shit I want," Klax said and spat at Kyan's feet. "Fuck you."

"I figured you'd say something like that," Kyan said, shaking his head before his eyes went past Klax. He opened his mouth and shouted, "Come on in, NuNu!"

"You can torture me all you want. I ain't agreei—"

"Klax!"

The tearful cry followed a door opening and shutting. It made Klax stop what he was saying in midsentence and finally, his poker face was broken. A tall, bulky man had entered the room, but he was not alone. He was dragging somebody with him. And that somebody was the one person in the world that Klax would die for.

"Kleigh," Klax whispered when NuNu tossed her roughly at his feet.

Her hair was all over the place, and when she looked tearfully up at him, he saw globs of blood under her nose. Her right eye was swollen with a broken blood vessel, and it was apparent that it would be black by evening. There were a few cuts on her quivering lips and the nape of her neck. Never in his life had he felt so broken, but seeing his baby sister like that tore him apart inside. It was all his fault. She wouldn't be in this predicament if it weren't for him. Tears welled in his eyes but didn't fall. The sorrow he felt for failing her was too much to bear.

"Klax, they k-k-killed Drop and the others," she was able to get out. "Whatever they want, don't tell them shit. They're gon' kill us anyway."

On her last words, NuNu snatched her by the back of her hair and dragged her back out of the room. Her screams of pain brought out Klax's screams of anger. He rocked the chair trying with all of his might to break free, but still couldn't. He clenched his teeth tightly, and if looks could kill, Kyan would have been dead ten times.

"Let her go," Klax growled. "Let her go! This shit don't have nothing to do with her, and you know it."

"It does if she's the only way that I can get what I want out of you," Kyan said, crossing one leg over the other and clasping his hands together. "You ready to cooperate now?"

Kleigh's beat-up face was stamped in Klax's mind. How could he have let things go so far and get so bad? He sat there, madder at himself than anyone else. Especially given the fact that he had the chance to kill Kyan once, but missed his target. Despite what Kleigh had just said, Klax knew he would do whatever he needed to, to save her, even if his attempts were futile. For the first time in life, Klax hung his head. When finally he lifted it, he stared into Kyan's pleased eyes and nodded his head.

"What you need me to do?"

"I just told you what I needed you to do. Now all you have to say is yes."

"It's more than me just stepping down from the position. Your plan is flawed."

"Is it?" Kyan said, raising his eyebrow in an intrigued manner. "Do enlighten me."

"You said yourself that I have too much clout, too much love, and too much respect throughout this whole state. Even if I weren't the king, I would still be the king. Plus, if I leave now, Harlem will seem weak, and the connect may pull all business."

"Well, how can we get around that then? Use that pretty boy head of yours—or I put your sister's on the chopping block."

"If you really want to take my place, you have to get in good with the connect."

"And how do you suggest that I do that?"

"The only way is to meet with the buyer," Klax said with a straight face.

"The buyer?"

"He's the only one the connect meets with alone. And then he distributes all of the product accordingly to every territory. If he says you're good, then you're good."

"A'ight, bet," Kyan said, pulling his phone out of his pocket. "Make the call."

"If it were that easy, don't you think somebody would have done that by now?" Klax said, shaking his head. "The buyer doesn't do personal phone calls. He only meets in person, at the spot and time of his choosing."

"And how do you get in contact with the buyer?"

"I already have a meeting set up two days from now, at a warehouse in downtown Manhattan at six o'clock. I, however, have to be there in one piece, or it's a no go."

Kyan eyed Klax scrupulously as if he were looking for a lie. Klax didn't blink once, and when Kyan was satisfied, he nodded. He stood up and slid the phone he was holding into the pocket of Klax's jeans.

"That's yours. Send me the location of the meeting spot. I'll be in touch."

"What about my sister?"

"She stays with me until you've held up your end of the bargain," Kyan said.

"The day of the meeting, if I don't see her there alive, I'm calling it off, and you can find another way to get what you want. Lay another hand on her, same deal. You understand me?"

"Well, looky here, even tied up and useless, you still got a little oomph in you, huh?" Kyan said with a chuckle and started toward the door. "You have my word. Don't do something stupid when you leave here, like trying to find your sister or me. I have eyes and ears everywhere right now. One false move and the girl is dead. Understand me?"

"I understand," Klax told him.

"Cut him loose!" Kyan shouted.

On command, the door opened, and five heavily armed men entered. One of them cut all of Klax's ties, except his hands, while the other put a bag over his head so that all he could see was darkness. He felt a gun press at the back of his head as he was forced to get up and walk. He didn't know where they were leading him, but when he felt the cold air on his upper body, he knew that he was back outside. However, he only felt the cold for a split second before he was thrown inside the trunk of a car. The entire ride he smelled the stomach-churning odor of a rotting corpse, and *that* told him that he was not the only body back there. If it weren't for the fact that the thought of him leaving Kleigh behind made him more nauseated than lying next to a rotting body, he was sure he would have been sick. Not only had he left her for dead, but he also didn't even know where "for dead" was. He'd spent all that time trying to keep her safe, and it turned out that not even he could do that.

The car stopped after about forty minutes of driving, and the trunk opened. The bag was snatched off his head, and one of the men who Klax recognized as NuNu punched him hard in the abdomen before snatching him out of the car and throwing him on the ground. They untied his hands, and they went straight to his stomach.

"You can walk the rest of the way, chump," he said with a malicious grin. "Soft-ass nigga. Come on, let's roll. Let this motherfucka freeze."

Klax was left holding his ribs when they sped off down the road. He wasn't even able to see what kind of car they were in, but that didn't matter because they would all have their day. Slowly, he stood to his feet and looked around. His body was weak, and he swayed a little bit. The sun had set, and he could hear the loud chirping of crickets all around him on the empty road. There were no houses within eyesight, nor were any cars driving by. Klax had no idea where he was. He felt his pocket and pulled the phone out of it. He then called the one person he knew would come through for him.

"Bro!" Adonis shouted when he answered the phone. "I've been calling you all fucking day! They got your crib on the news. I thought . . . I thought you were gone, man."

"He has Kleigh," was all Klax could say.

"He what? Who's 'he'?"

"The same nigga that set Tron up. He got to Kleigh somehow," Klax told him. "I'm about to send you my location. These niggas dropped me off on the side of the road in the middle of nowhere. I need you to come get me. I'ma kill all of 'em."

"I'm on my way, and oh! This might not be the best time to mention it but—"

"Give me this phone, nigga," Klax heard a voice in the background say.

"You ain't gotta snatch," Adonis said, his voice sounding a little further in the background now.

"Yeah, whatever. Hello?" the voice said into the phone.

"Tron?" Klax asked to be sure he wasn't hearing things.

"In the flesh," Tron said. "Why you send this hood Carlton up to the prison to get me instead of you?"

"I was a little wrapped up with some things. How'd he get you out?"

"Apparently, homeboy went to my place and found the surveillance camera I hid in a cookie jar. I've always been a paranoid kind of nigga. You should see the security setup at my spot in Albany. I ain't really have time to do all that here, so I did the nanny cam thing. Anyway, the footage showed one of my old hitters Nushawn planting the bombs there while I was gone. They had no choice but to release me. They tried to keep a nigga another night, but Adonis came down and showed his ass at the jail."

"Nushawn," Klax inquired. "NuNu?"

"Yup. And your crib has his handiwork written all over it," Tron told him. "Aye, where the fuck you been? We been tryna reach you since I got out."

"Kyan had his goons snatch me up," Klax said.

"And you're still breathing?"

"For now," Klax said.

"Why did he let you go?"

"I have something he wants, and he has someone I love," Klax said.

Kyan didn't know that what he thought was a simple chess move wasn't. He had completely changed the game when he took Kleigh. The difference in their positions was that Kyan might have wanted what Klax had, but Klax needed Kleigh. One of them spoke higher volumes.

"He got Kleigh?" Tron's voice raised in alarm.

"Yeah, he got her," Klax said, and he heard his voice crack. "He got to my baby sister, man. And if I don't give him what he wants, he's gon' kill her."

"I ain't gon' let that happen."

"Me either. And that's why I'm gon' give him what he wants," Klax said matter-of-factly.

"What does he want? Money? More product?"

"Nah. He wants me."

"What? You ain't making no sense. He just had you."

"He had me as Klax, the kingpin of Harlem."

"Bro . . . I'm lost. What the fuck are you talking about?"

"I'll explain when y'all come swoop me. Pull up. I'm sending my location now."

"No doubt. We're on the way."

Chapter 16

"There is no such thing as helplessness. It's just another word for giving up."
—Jefferson Smith

Kleigh

"Get the fuck off of me!" Kleigh screamed at the jolt of pain coming from her head as the man named NuNu dragged her.

She screamed and shouted for her brother continuously and tried her hardest to get back to him. However, kicking her feet and clawing at NuNu's hands seemed futile because he was just too strong. He dragged her by her hair all the way back to the room he'd pulled her from, and when they were there, he shoved her hard to the ground.

"Damn, we fucked you up good, and you still want to fight, shorty? I like you," he said and blew her a menacing kiss. "I'ma see if the boss will let me have some fun with you tonight after all this."

He shut the door and locked it before she had a chance to get back up. She stumbled to the door and let her fists bang on it until they were numb. She had no more energy. She thought about Klax, her mother, Bahli, and Tron. She didn't know if she'd get to see any of them again. She screamed until her screams turned to sobs and until her sobs turned to silence. Slapping the door one more time, she slid down to the floor and crawled back over to her cot.

Cold and curled in a fetal position, Kleigh tried to make herself comfortable on the small cot, but it was impossible. She was accustomed to a higher way of living, not that of a dog. Her entire body ached, and she couldn't help but think that maybe trying to fight off grown men with guns wasn't a good idea, especially when they ended up getting what they wanted anyway. But at the time, she didn't know what they wanted, and her will to survive kicked in. Now, there she was with a busted up face and aching ribs. She didn't have the slightest idea where she was. All she knew was that it was freezing because she was still in her pajamas.

The cot she lay on was on the concrete ground, and the walls around her were dirty. The lightbulb on the ceiling was dim and barely gave any light. The only thing she was given for warmth was a smelly blanket that she wouldn't dare use even if there were a blizzard blowing in her room. Instead, she lay with her knees to her chest and tried to keep herself warm. The room was the same size as a college dorm, and Kleigh's eyes stayed on the tall door, hoping that it would open and let out some of the musty air. There were no windows, so Kleigh didn't know if it was night or day, but she knew she'd been gone for almost five hours . . . or maybe it was six. She'd been stripped of every device she had, even the watch on her wrist, so she didn't know what time it was.

Kleigh wasn't alone in the room either. There was one other person in the far corner lying on a cot like hers. She, however, was wrapped up in the nasty blanket she was given like it was nothing. Kleigh hadn't said a word to her in the hours she'd been there. She hadn't even looked at her face to see who she was and what she looked like. She just felt her presence lingering in the darkness. All Kleigh wanted to do was get out of there. She knew that Klax was worried sick about her. She wondered if he knew his watchmen were dead.

"Hey," the other girl said in a soft, quiet voice. She had interrupted Kleigh's thoughts, and although Kleigh had heard her, she remained silent. The girl didn't take the hint that Kleigh didn't want to speak and said, "*Psst!*"

"What?" Kleigh snapped still facing the wall.

"Depending on how long you're here, you'll get used to the dirty blankets," the girl said. "I'm Cali, by the way, what's your name?"

"Why?"

"Because we're in here together and might as well make small talk to pass the time."

"Well, I'm just fine with being quiet. We don't need to get to know each other."

"Oh," Cali said in a disappointed tone. "I'm sorry. I've just been here by myself for a while. I didn't talk to you at first because I thought they had knocked you out when they tossed you in here."

"How long have you been here?" Kleigh asked, suddenly curious.

"I lost count after two weeks, but if I had to guess, I would have to say a little over a month now."

"And they just keep you locked up in here like a dog?"

"Nah, not usually. I did something bad the other night, and Kyan is punishing me for it."

"That's who has my brother here. I think . . . I think he's going to kill him."

"I wouldn't put it past him," Cali said sympathetically. "I'm here because my pimp owed him a lot of money for the product he gave us working girls to do what we do. So, Kyan took me and Ron's, that's my pimp, other best girl as collateral until he paid his debt."

"Where is she?"

"Dead," Cali said without flinching. "Kyan killed her. Shot her right in the head in front of me. I thought Ron would have come to get me by now, but he hasn't. I don't think he cares."

"Well, he's a pimp. I'm sure he's replaced you by now," Kleigh said flatly and then sighed. "I'm sorry. That was mean. I'm just dealing with a lot inside right now. I've never felt so helpless in my life."

Flashes of Klax bound in the chair plagued her mind. She didn't know what happened when she was dragged out of the room, and there was a big lump in the back of her throat. She wouldn't want to live if Klax were murdered.

"Nah, you're good, boo. You're probably right. That's why I've been just trying to get used to my life here. I don't have anybody else, and when I'm a good girl, Kyan lets me stay in nice hotel rooms. He has me turning tricks for him now, setting niggas up type shit."

"So what did you do to end up in here?"

"I let one of my tricks get away. He caught on to what I was doing and overpowered me over at the Hilton. Kyan wasn't happy about it at all. H-he hurt me. And locked me in this room with no food and barely any water."

"Are you able to go to the bathroom?" Kleigh said, turning to face her.

Cali was sitting up with her back against the wall behind her. Her long, messy hair hung over her shoulders, and Kleigh could make out a few bruises on her neck and face. Cali looked tired, like she barely had any energy to move, but she offered Kleigh a kind smile when she saw her turn her way.

"Yes. I knock on the door and ask permission," Cali said, and Kleigh saw her shoulders move like she didn't think it was a big deal.

"Permission?"

"Yup. They escort me and take me to go handle my business. I can show you all of the ropes if you'd like. Kyan is the kind of man whose bad side you don't want to see. And if you're here and still alive, he must see something in you that can bring him money."

Kleigh recognized something in Cali's voice that she hadn't heard since her father was on his deathbed. It was the same tone he had when he told her goodbye: not hopelessness, but defeat. Cali had accepted her fate and was just playing the card dealt to her, but Kleigh couldn't be like that. She refused. She was so taken aback by how Cali was talking like what was happening to them was normal, because it wasn't, and it wouldn't become her reality.

"They deadass took your freedom, and you're not mad at all? You're just OK with living like this until Kyan doesn't have any more use for you?"

"Why shouldn't I be? I'd rather be here than on the streets hooking for myself, getting beat up, and robbed every other day."

"If that's how you feel, but I won't be like that."

"You'll be surprised how easy it is to be broken."

"Nah. Not me. M-my brother is going to get free and come save me. So, no, I don't need you to 'show me the ropes' because I won't be here much longer."

"You sure about that?"

Kleigh's eyes went from Cali to the locked door, and she felt hot tears come to her eyes. A strong sorrow overcame her as the realization that she probably wasn't getting out of there set in on her. She'd never seen Klax battered or broken, and that shattered her heart. Kleigh's chin dropped to her chest, and she began to sob heavily.

"I'm sorry," she heard Cali say when Kleigh's sobs grew quieter.

"Me too," Kleigh whispered.

Chapter 17

"The best weapon against my enemy is another enemy."
—Friedrich Nietzsche

Tron

Klax's lawyer had done the work of a miracle for Tron, and for that, he would forever be in Klax's debt. He didn't have to look out, especially given the fact that he had caused so much trouble for him, but he looked out. And so now, it was his turn to return the favor. He was going to help Klax bring back peace to Harlem once and for all. After picking up Klax and taking him to the ER to make sure he didn't have any broken bones or any other long-term damage, they all went back to Adonis's place.

It was three in the morning, and the three men sat in Adonis's dining room around his table, along with Kleigh's best friend, Bahli. Upon hearing about Kleigh's kidnapping, she refused to go home and wait for them to figure things out, and Tron couldn't blame her. It would take all of their combined power to bring her home safely. But to do that, they would all need to be levelheaded, and that was what Tron was struggling with.

"I'm gon' go blow off all their heads, and that's my word," he said after Klax mentioned Kleigh's bruised face.

"And we will," Klax told him. "But, first, we need a plan."

"Well, what can I do?" Bahli asked him. "Kleigh has been my girl since I can remember. If something happens to her, I don't know what I'll do."

"Something already happened to her," Tron said. "The longer we wait, the more at risk she becomes."

"Nah, Kyan ain't gon' do nothing to her," Klax said.

"You don't know him like I do." Tron shook his head. "His heart is colder than any nigga I've ever met."

"That may be true, but he knows if he hurts her, then the deal is off."

"OK, so, then, what?" Adonis asked. "What's the move?"

"Yeah, G. What's this shit you were talking on the phone?" Tron asked, furrowing his brow at Klax. "You said what Kyan wants is you. If that's the case, why did he let you go?"

"Kyan wants a meeting with the buyer, and I'm the only one who can set that up."

"The buyer as in . . .?"

"Every hustler in New York's connect to the connect," Adonis spoke up.

"Why you ain't just set that up while he had you?" Tron asked. He watched Adonis and Klax exchange a look. "I'm obviously missing something. What is it?"

"Klax *is* the buyer," Adonis said, making Tron's mouth drop slightly. "I just found out myself. Don't look so shocked."

"And Kyan doesn't know that, which gives me an advantage. Now, we need to figure out what to do with that advantage."

"Nah, we not about to fly by that like you ain't just say what you said. *You're* the buyer? That means you're like the baby connect."

"Baby connect?" Klax made a face.

"You know what I mean, nigga. This means, I was tryna kill the nigga I was tryna link with, because the nigga I was tryna link with after I killed you, was *you!* This shit is confusing, G."

"Don't think too hard about it," Adonis told him. "We need that brain power for the issues at hand. You can get Klax's autograph later."

"Nigga, I'll—"

"Hello!" Bahli said and waved her hands in the air. "Stop ego clashing and let's get back to it. My bitch needs to be back home where she belongs. Period. I'm not about to play with these niggas! So I need to know what y'all need me to do. Set a nigga up? Follow somebody? Shoot somebody? I ain't never did it before, but I ain't scared."

Something she said sparked Tron's attention. Since he'd met Kleigh, Tron could honestly say he hadn't looked at another woman as anything but that. As in, he didn't even take in her features because, in his mind, nothing compared to Kleigh. But right then, he saw Bahli as the beautiful woman she was. So beautiful that any man could unknowingly fall into her trap.

Any man like NuNu.

"Aye," Tron said, looking at Klax. "I have an idea."

"What you thinking?"

"What do you say we hit them from the front *and* the back?"

"Explain."

"You said that where they had you was where you think they were keeping Kleigh, right?"

"That's right."

"Then we just need to figure out where that's at."

"How we gon' do that? I told you that I had a bag over my head. I ain't see shit."

"What's every nigga's kryptonite?" Tron asked.

"Money," Klax said.

"No."

"Power?" Adonis tried.

"No again."

"Pussy," Bahli answered.

"Exactly," Tron said. "I know a gentlemen's spot in Albany that our friend NuNu can't seem to stay out of. A girl I used to know back in the day works there. She can help us plant an inside man . . . or woman."

All three men's eyes fell on Bahli, and then she rolled hers.

"So, y'all niggas deadass want me to be a stripper?"

"We just need you to use that charm of yours and find out the location of where they're holding Kleigh," Klax said. "We ain't gon' ever be too far away from you."

"Now why would he tell me some top secret information like that?"

"You'd be surprised what the allure of pussy can do," Adonis said, and the two of them shared a look. "I mean, shit, look at me. You got me wide open over here, girl."

"Adonis, don't gas me up. You know I like running on E."

"Nah, ain't no gas, shorty. I'm pumping the brakes right now because I'm telling you the truth," he said. "You got that kind of shit that will make a nigga shell out his soul. How do you think you got me in the first place?"

"Got you?" she asked with a small smile.

"Yeah," Adonis smiled back. "But do you got me?"

"You know I do," Bahli said and sighed and shook her head, turning her attention to Tron. "But I got my girl more. Adonis told me about how you were playing my bitch at first. How do I know I can trust you?"

"I wouldn't be here if you couldn't," Tron told her. "And I wouldn't be sitting here at this table attempting to help come up with a plan to bring her home either. I ain't gon' cap about my initial intentions, but it looks like fate knew what it was doing by letting me fall into her clutches. And now that I'm there, I'm not gon' let her let me go. Or vice versa. God ain't bless me with the presence of a woman like Kleigh to let a nigga like Kyan take her away from me so easily. So I'm gon' get her back, even if that means going to war, guns blazing by myself."

"You love her?" Bahli asked curiously.

"I'm falling," Tron answered.

"Mmm," Bahli said, pursing her lips. "You lucky that I know for a fact that she's falling for your cute ass too. All right, fuck it. What all I gotta do?"

Chapter 18

"Courage is doing what you're afraid to do."
—Eddie Rickenbacker

Bahli

"Drip too hard, don't stand too close. You gon' fuck around and drown off this wave!" Lil Baby's voice filled the packed gentlemen's club, Rose Petals, and thousands of one-dollar bills fell from the sky and onto the stage. The woman on the pole was working for the money and moving her body like a pro. She wore a black thong teddy that showcased her thick backside and wide hips. Then a pair of six-inch, open-toe heels made her sit up in all of the right places as she worked the stage like it was the last performance she'd ever have. In truth, she hoped it was. Bahli whipped her hair over her shoulder and looked back at the large crowd around the stage, catcalling her. Quiet as kept, Bahli had danced a few times in her late teenage years. She had never been the type to ask for a handout even though her best friend was paid. Bahli was the type to go out and get it herself, by any means necessary. She knew she was there for a reason, but seeing all the money being thrown her way, she was for sure taking it all home with her.

So far, she was the only girl that the crowd was going crazy for, but that was part of the scheme. Klax had paid all of the other dancers a pretty penny to be nothing short of mediocre that night. That way, Bahli could stand out. If he had known that she could work the pole like that, he would have saved his money.

"Let's give a round of applause for Honey Dip!" The DJ shouted into the microphone when the song was over.

Bahli slid around on the floor of the stage sweeping her money into a big pile with her hands and arms. She purposely crawled seductively by a small group of men standing to the far right of the stage. NuNu probably thought she was coming his way because he had a handful of hundreds, but really, it was because she had finally spotted her mark. Standing there wearing Gucci from head to toe and rocking a fresh haircut, NuNu was all smiles. He was more handsome than his photo, with his smooth, chocolate skin and radiant white smile, but knowing who he really was made him as ugly as could be. Still, when Bahli got close to him, she gave him her sexiest cat eyes.

"Is that for me, baby boy?" she asked seductively talking about the money in his hand.

"That depends on what you're tryna do for it," he said and let his eyes fall on her cleavage.

"Is that right?"

"You know that's right, girl," he said, licking his lips. "You were on fire up there. Let me get a private dance."

"I got you," Bahli told him with a wink. "Let me go to the back and put my money up and meet me in room five, OK?"

"Bet."

Moments later, Bahli's heart was pounding as she made her way back to the dressing room with a large bag of money. She glanced behind her, and in the distance, she saw that NuNu wasted no time in heading up to the private room. Before she could turn her head front facing again, she felt someone grab her arm as she passed the bar. She was about to smack the daylights out of whoever it was, but when she saw that it was Adonis, she relaxed. He was sitting at the bar sipping a drink and blending in with the crowd. She felt a wave of relief, just knowing he was there.

"You good?" he asked.

"Yes, I'm fine," she nodded. "That seemed too easy."

"Probably because it looks like you've done this before," he said with a smirk. "'Honey Dip'?"

"That was my name back when I had to do what I had to do to get by," she told him. "I haven't always been the *classy* woman you've come to know and care about."

"Well, shit, I'ma need to have a meeting with Honey Dip after this," he joked with a grin.

"I hate you," she said and cut her eyes at him.

"No, you don't," he said with a wink.

"Where's Klax?"

"Somewhere being a ghost. Go handle your business. Remember, get that location."

"I got it, I got it," she said and handed him the bag of money. "I need that. Don't lose it."

"You don't need this when you got me," Adonis said in all seriousness. "After this, I want to have a talk with you about some shit, but, yeah, you don't need this. Money ain't gon' be an issue for you anymore."

"Boy, bye. You *just* got out of a serious relationship. You ain't tryna bust no real moves with me," Bahli said and rolled her eyes. "We *just* spent our first full day together, and you see how *that* ended—with me on a damn stripper pole."

"And that's why I fuck with you. You ride for your people. That's what I need around me. If Tron and Kleigh can be falling in love so fast, why can't I try to move in that direction with you? And we been fucking around for way longer than them."

"You gotta show me that I'm more than just pussy to you, Adonis," Bahli told him with her hand on her hip.

"And I will. Whatever is in this bag of money," he said and held it up, "I'ma match it times two *and* take you somewhere distant to spend it. But in the meantime, here; take this."

He handed her the drink in front of him, and she was thankful for something to take the edge off. When she went to put it to her lips, Adonis snatched it away with wide eyes. He glanced around to make sure no one had seen the exchange.

"That ain't for you, girl!" he exclaimed. "You ain't never heard of 'don't drink on the job'? That's for your friend up there. Tron said he likes cranberry and vodka, and, well, this shit right here has a little bit extra fizzle in it . . . If you know what I mean. Go on."

Bahli understood completely what he meant and was happy that she hadn't even gotten a sip. She nodded her head and took the drink from him, more discreetly this time. When she turned around, he smacked her booty and put a couple of dollars on her garter for effect.

She then continued the rest of the way to the dressing room, working her way through the crowd to freshen up before heading up to the private dance rooms. The hallway leading to the rooms was lit up by red lights, giving a real sultry vibe. Each room had different music coming from it as she passed, but when she got to room five, all she heard was silence. She took a breath before she twisted the knob and walked inside. Sure enough, NuNu was sitting patiently on a black leather futon with a stack of money beside him. The moment he saw her enter, he smiled big. His eyes were low, so she knew he was already lifted off something, and she hoped that meant he wouldn't question the drink in her hand.

"Here you go," she said and handed it to him. "The bartender said this is one of your favorites."

"You tryna loosen me up so you can take all my money, huh?" he asked instantly taking a sip of the drink. He made a face, and Bahli's heart stopped for a moment. "Aaah! They know I like my shit strong. That's why I fuck with them. Turn on some music. I wanna feel that ass move on me."

Bahli let out the breath she was holding and went to the small MP3 player connected to the speaker on the side of the small room. She started to play some Cardi B, but he shook his head.

"Nah, play something slow. You gon' kill the vibe, shorty."

"I got you," she said and instead, opted for some Jacquees.

Slowly, she began to move her body to the singer's voice as NuNu sipped his drink. She wished he would just down it, but since he didn't, she bought herself as much time as possible. Turning so that he could get a good view of her rear end, she began twerking to the beat. She felt her thighs wiggle with her butt cheeks, and he threw a handful of hundreds at her. She couldn't lie . . . When the money touched her skin, it made her want to shake what her mama gave her even harder. Bahli stood up and danced seductively toward him. When she was close enough, she rotated her hips in his face while stroking the top of his head sensually.

"You think I'm sexy?"

"Hell yeah," he said.

"While I'm dancing, I want you to imagine your dick deep inside my pussy, okay?"

"A'ight," he breathed, looking up at her with lustful and longing eyes.

She sat down on his lap with her back facing him and grinded on his crotch. She felt his thickness through his pants and couldn't help getting turned on. That was a part that Adonis didn't need to know about. She enjoyed the feeling of NuNu's hard penis rubbing against her clit through the thin fabric of her clothes, and she even let him fondle her a little bit.

"You had a nigga's dick on swole the whole time you were on that pole," he whispered in her ear as she grinded on him. "I just had to have you."

"Is that right?" she purred. "Why is that?"

"You're the sexiest girl I've ever seen in this bitch. When did you start working here?"

"I'm new," she told him. "I just got in from out of town and needed some extra cash."

"Shit, you don't even need to be doing all this, shorty. Let a real nigga take care of you," he said, wrapping his arms around her waist. "If you were mine, you wouldn't need for nothing."

"Uh-huh," she said and tried not to gag from the powerful smell of liquor on his breath. "What kind of job you got where you think you can save me?"

"I'm a hustler, baby," NuNu told her and grabbed another handful of hundreds. He held them up and let them fall over her breasts and into her lap. "And there's more where this came from."

"Mmm-hmm," Bahli said. "That's what you're saying."

She felt herself starting to panic again. The song was almost over, and NuNu was still very much conscious. Not only that, but his hands kept inching to the place in between her legs. If he thought he was really going to get to sleep with her, he had another think coming.

"That's what I know," he said and tightened his grip on her. "Now, all you have to do is give me a little sample, and I got you."

"I don't think I have to do anything but dance."

When she tried to get up, NuNu pulled her back down on him.

"Nah, I just threw some bands at that ass. I'm finna get some pussy," he said, pulling the crotch part of her teddy to the side and exposed her second set of lips. He had a grip so tight around her arms and upper body that she couldn't move. "I knew this shit was gon' be phat."

He squeezed it in his hand first and then forced two fingers inside of her. NuNu's fingers thrust a few times before he pulled them out and brought them to his mouth.

"Mmm, and it taste good too," he said and tossed her on the futon.

"No!" She tried to get up again, but that time in a drunken daze, he smacked her down.

"Bitch, stay down. I said you're about to give me some pussy."

She held her mouth and tasted blood from her busted bottom lip. That's not how things were supposed to go. He was too strong, and she couldn't overpower him even if she tried. The club was too loud, and she knew if she screamed, nobody would hear her anyway. NuNu stood over her and pulled down his pants, exposing his giant dick to her. Just as he was leaning down to have sex with her . . . He stumbled. Bahli watched him blink his eyes hard and try to shake off whatever feeling had overcome him, but he just stumbled again. She sat up and scooted to the far end of the futon as she watched the drugs finally begin to take effect on him. He fell to the ground, on his side, with his pants down, out like a light. Bahli used her heel to poke him to make sure he was really down for the count, and when he didn't move, she hopped into action. She fixed her teddy and went to rummage in his pants pockets for his cell phone.

"Bingo," she said when she found it and began scrolling through his messages.

It wasn't hard to pinpoint which number belonged to Kyan since it was the only number NuNu had saved in his phone. She scrolled their message thread until she found what she was looking for. There was a text message from the morning that Kleigh had gotten taken that caught her attention.

Kyan: You grab the girl?

NuNu: Yea.

Kyan: Wait for the drop spot.

Bahli scrolled down once more and saw that Kyan sent the address to the place where NuNu was supposed to take Kleigh. Her hands were shaking as she screen shot the message and sent it to Adonis. She deleted all the evidence showing she'd been in his phone and placed it back in his pocket. Before she left, Bahli grabbed all of the money NuNu had brought to the private dance room and spit in his face on her way out the door. She knew he would just assume that she was a trifling stripper who had gotten the one up on him and robbed him when he finally came to. But by then, she would be long gone. Bahli had done her part. Now, it was time for Phase Two.

Chapter 19

"Sometimes you have to get lost to find your way."
—Anonymous

Klax

It was hard for Klax to do much of anything with Kleigh in the predicament she was in. His mother was suspicious about why Kleigh wasn't answering her phone calls, and Klax just told her it was because she was dealing with a few things and wanted to be left alone. However, his mother wasn't green, and he knew that excuse would only work for so long, especially with what had happened to his home. He had to stop answering her calls as well. He had too much on his mind and at stake to be sidetracked.

Bahli had come through on the information they needed, and when Adonis gave him the address, it was hard for Klax not to jump the gun. He wanted to send a street army in and make as much noise as possible, but it was chess, not checkers. Every move had to be calculated. In order to clear his head of the millions of thoughts running through it, Klax decided to take a walk through Harlem. He parked his Range Rover, which had suffered some damage from the detonation, in front of an apartment dwelling and got out. It was cold outside, but as soon as he stepped foot on the concrete, he felt the warmth of protection set in. While in Harlem, he was untouchable. He was at home when he was there. Klax had cleaned up Harlem the best that he could and had even opened a clinic for the junkies. It used to make him feel better knowing that he didn't sell directly to the junkies on the streets, but then again, it didn't matter if the drugs came straight from his hands. They were still his drugs.

The dope game had always played tug-of-war with Klax's conscience. How could he poison his people, yet try to help them at the same time? It was equivalent to an abusive relationship where one partner would break the other down so that they were the one who could build them back up. As much as he tried to not be like his father, there was one piece of his old man that would always be embedded in him. And that was the love for money. The increments Klax saw on a daily was what gassed him. The dollar flow made that tug-of-war game worth it. He didn't know if he could ever really be like Sunny and get out of the game because whereas it was a gamble, while Klax was playing, he had the power to make a real difference. And if somebody clipped him in the process, he would die knowing that all his bad had been matched with a lot of good.

As he walked early that morning, he felt the sun on his face. There was a lot that could go wrong later in the evening, but if he played his cards right, it wouldn't be on his end. In the past weeks, he'd suffered many losses, and anyone else in his position would have been furious and ready to catch as many bodies as possible. He was angry at the material things he lost, but not to the point where he couldn't take that misfortune with a grain of salt and put it to the back of his mind. Up until his sister was taken, he hadn't lost anything that he couldn't replace. None of that was irreplaceable, including the theater. Some may look at his lack of retaliation as weak, but that was because their value of time was not the same. To Klax, his enemies always lost if he still had breath in him. They wasted their time making moves to hurt him without knowing the full circumference of the circle. They attacked him because they wanted his seat, but they would always fail because the seat they went after was the wrong seat. Klax hadn't even begun to dig into his bag of tricks, but soon, Kyan would understand why he was an ultimate king.

"Kevin Turner?"

The deep baritone came from close behind and interrupted Klax's morning walk. He turned around and found himself face-to-face with two tall, white men. Detectives. He recognized one of them as the man who had arrested Tron, and Klax smirked at the displeased look on his face.

"I'm Detective Hanes," the blond-haired man said and pointed at his partner with the bald head. "And this is Detective Terry. Are you Keven Turner?"

"You asking that like you don't know it's me," Klax said. "Especially since I know you must be the detectives digging your noses in all of my affairs."

"We didn't know if it was really you, or if we were seeing a ghost, especially since your house went up in flames a few days ago," Detective Terry said. "It caused quite the frenzy in that quiet neighborhood you lived in. I see that Range Rover of yours looks like it got messed up pretty badly."

"Material can always be replaced. Anything else? I got better shit to do than to look in your pale-ass faces."

"We see you got your friend out of jail," Detective Terry said before Klax could turn away. "Funny thing is that when we asked him about you, he said he didn't know you. All charges against him were mysteriously dropped.

I wonder how that happened. How much money did you have to spend to work that kind of magic?"

"Not a dime when a man is innocent," Klax said, not missing a beat. "When I heard of another black man wrongfully arrested by the police, my legal advisor got right on it. The last time I checked, that wasn't a crime. I have the best lawyer in New York, and he just worked fast. Not to mention the video caught by one of the officers on scene caught your dumb ass punching a man in handcuffs who wasn't resisting arrest. You should be thanking my lawyer. He just asked for the marijuana charge to be dropped instead of you losing your job. Can you imagine the uproar, especially in this social media age, if that video would have got out? You're welcome. Now, get the fuck off my block before something *really* happens to you."

"Is that a threat?" Detective Hanes said, angrily glaring at Klax.

Detective Terry's eyes weren't on Klax, however. His were on the twenty-something men that had stepped out of the shadows all around them. He cleared his throat to get his partner's attention, but Detective Hanes ignored him.

"You think you're untouchable, boy?" He sneered and took a step toward Klax, who smirked.

"Nah, but here in Harlem? I am."

Detective Terry grabbed Detective Hanes firmly by the shoulder to get his attention. When Detective Hanes finally looked, his partner pointed at the menacing eyes watching them.

"You think I'm scared of a bunch of thugs? They'll be locked up in minutes fucking with me."

"They'd have to find your bodies first to stick a charge," Klax said simply, but the threat lingered in the air like a horrible stench.

Detective Terry tugged his partner back so they could return to their undercover vehicle. Detective Hanes went without a fight, but not before getting one last word in.

"This ain't over, boy."

"It is, trust me," Klax said, looking him square in the eye. "Tell me something, Detectives, are y'all only good cops when you're tryna get recognized? Y'all ain't the only ones with ears in the streets, and a little birdie told me all about Starsky & Hutch. After I found out you two were digging up information about me, I took the liberty of doing the same about you. I know that you, Hanes, extort the Vatos Locos in the Bronx threatening them with jail time if they don't cooperate. How do you think the department will feel knowing you've been taking drug money? And I know that you, Terry, got a pregnant bitch in Manhattan. How do you think your wife will feel about that? She would take you for everything, huh?"

The looks of shock on their faces were priceless. Once again, it was chess, not checkers. To defeat one's enemies, sometimes, using might doesn't always do the trick. Sometimes, you have to use your resources and save your strength for a more important fight.

"Don't get caught over here again. They don't see badges over this way; only the faces of those who don't belong."

He didn't care to indulge in any further conversation with the detectives. He turned his back to them and continued on his walk around the block. In the distance, he saw Dame sitting on the hood of an old-school Impala smoking a blunt. They connected eyes, and he gave Klax a head nod before turning his attention back to the detectives. Behind him, Klax heard the soft purr of an engine, and seconds later, he saw the Dodge drive past him and off his territory. Klax didn't doubt that he wouldn't be seeing those detectives for a while and that he'd gotten them off his coattail. Maybe not for forever, but for a while, at least.

Whenever Klax needed to decipher his thoughts, a walk around Harlem did it. Starsky & Hutch had interrupted the process, but in a way, they had helped him. It reminded him that hundreds of lives would be willing to lie down to preserve his. And whereas he knew Kyan wouldn't come to Harlem—that would be a suicide mission—Klax could bring Harlem to him. Maybe not in physical form, because for Klax, war and casualties were always the final resort, but in spirit. Just like that, he knew which trick he wanted to pull out of the bag. He grinned to himself and shouted over to his street general.

"Yo, Dame! Come holler at me for a second."

Chapter 20

"Some of the greatest battles will be fought within the silent chambers of your own soul."

—Ezra Taft Benson

Kyan

The night he had been waiting on for what felt like his entire life had finally arrived. Ma'Kyan Blount had been number two for as long as he could remember. He had grown up in a small town on the outskirts of Houston, Texas, born to a middle-class couple, Patricia and Ma'Kyan Blount Sr. He came into the world as a number two, and that meant he was always in his father's shadow. No matter what he did, he didn't do it as good as his dad. Even if he thought he did a great job.

"I was great in math. Get that B up to an A."
"I had better form when I shot my jumper; go practice until your hands bleed."
"Sit up straight; you don't see me slouching, do you?"

The list went on and on. It wasn't the pressure that got to Kyan. It was the constant comparisons. Nobody saw him as his own person. He was just an extension of the man that had come before him. When his mother died suddenly of a heart attack at an early age, he desperately needed to be his father's number one for once. He was only 17 at the time and had never dealt with a pain so severe, but his father was too busy trying to replace her to make Kyan a priority. She hadn't been in the dirt for a year by the time Kyan's father got remarried to a woman named Carla. She was beautiful, and ten years Ma'Kyan Sr.'s junior. But he was head over heels. Kyan often wondered that if his father knew she had a thing for "number twos," would he have gone forward with the marriage.

The first time Kyan slept with his dad's new wife was when he was out of school on break. Back then, his father worked long hours for an electric company, so that meant Kyan and Carla often spent a lot of alone time together. A few times, Kyan had noticed Carla give him extras during mealtime or had come check on him a few times throughout the night. He thought it was because she was trying to do the "motherly thing," but in truth, she wanted to be anything else *but* a mother to him. She took Kyan's virginity, and the two of them continued a secret relationship for a year. For once in his life, he had someone who made him feel like number one, and he fell in love with her. On his eighteenth birthday, he was going to ask her to run away with him, but his father walked in on them in the act before he could pose the question.

"Carla, what the hell are you doing?" Ma'Kyan shouted when he saw his wife riding Kyan like a rodeo queen in Kyan's small bedroom.

The look of detest frozen on his face made Kyan afraid to come from under the covers on his full-sized bed. His father's gaze went back and forth from him to Carla. The two lovers thought that he was supposed to work late, but there he was . . . home early.

"Baby, I can explain," Carl said, grabbing her robe and wrapping it around her before she got up from the bed.

Kyan felt his limp penis slide out of her when she climbed off of him and reached for his underwear and pants while she tried to calm his father down.

"Explain what? There ain't shit to explain! You're fucking my son!"

"Baby, I'm so sorry," Carla pleaded with him and placed the soft hands Kyan loved so much on Ma'Kyan's chest. "I just get so lonely here by myself. You work so much, and when you get home, you don't have any time for me. And, well, Kyan looks so much like you to me. I couldn't help myself. I'm sorry. Please don't leave me. I don't know what I'll do without you."

"And what do you have to say about this shit, boy? You're too much of a little bitch to get your own woman? I house you and clothe you, and this is how you repay me? You gotta get your shit and get the hell up out of here! I don't ever want to see you again. You ain't no son of mine!" Ma'Kyan shouted and turned back to Carla. "And you? I'll deal with you later. Go to our bedroom."

"Carla?" Kyan asked with a confused expression on his face. "He's kicking me out. Aren't you gonna come with me? I thought you loved me."

"I can't love a boy who can't even provide shelter or pay a bill," Carla said, looking him square in the eyes. "I love your father. Now you heard him—get out."

Kyan hadn't felt a hurt like that since the loss of his mother, and it sent him into a rage. Once again, he was just number two. He left, but his anger caused him to come back and set fire to the house, killing the couple in their sleep. The fire was ruled as an electrical freak accident, and since Kyan was 18, he was free to go where he pleased.

He only had the clothes on his back and enough money for a bus ticket. He didn't know why at the time, but he chose New York, and that would prove to be the best decision he ever made. There, he met Arnold "Sunny" Walker, a young street hustler. They called him Sunny because he shed light wherever he went, and that's what he did when he found Kyan sleeping on a bench. Sunny not only put him on with the crew he was running with, but he gave Kyan half of the clothes in his wardrobe and a warm bed to sleep in. They were thick as thieves and grew in ranks together. Kyan had finally found an equal, and he was happy with that. They worked under a big-time hustler named Baller doing runs and hitting licks for him. It kept money in their pockets and food in their stomachs, and at the time, that was enough for them. However, there was something about Sunny that Baller saw in him that he didn't see in Kyan.

Over the years, Kyan watched Sunny rise to the top, and although Sunny never left Kyan behind, he was right back to being number two. Kyan didn't know when the seed of poison was planted in his spirit toward his best friend, but it was long before he sent Kameron to his home. That day was just the moment Kyan knew his heart had gone completely black. He didn't feel anything at the loss of the woman he'd grown to call a sister or the little girl he claimed to love like a niece. All he cared about was finally being number one. Kyan thought that although Sunny had survived, it would be easy to take his spot. However, he had underestimated Kameron's claim to the streets. When Sunny went down, their most loyal switched sides and left Kyan with no army, no workers, and no clientele. He was forced to uproot his life and move with the man he had set up.

Sunny grew content with the life of a normal man, but Kyan couldn't get the thirst of the fast money out of his system. He didn't just want one territory; he wanted them all. The streets sang to him like a siren to a sailor at sea. The hunger that he felt in himself manifested in a boy he was entrusted to care for. LaTron looked up to him, more than his father. And finally, he was somebody's number one. Still, the feeling of fondness for the boy didn't stop him from planting the seed of hatred toward Kameron, although he knew it really should have been toward him. He was the one who pointed Tron in the direction of revenge, but in reality, he just wanted the boy to do what he couldn't. And when the deed was over, so would his need for Tron.

Kyan knew that he could have easily just told Tron about what he wanted to do, but he didn't want the boy to tell Sunny. Not only that, but in the end, Kyan didn't want to share. It was enough having Tron think that he called the shots in Albany. Kyan molded Tron into the perfect soldier but took note of all his weaknesses. Sunny being number one. Tron's father was all the family he had left, and Kyan knew he wasn't built to be in the world alone. By killing Sunny and taking back the army he'd lent, Tron had nothing and nobody. He was defeated. The thought of him alone and lost in his own regretful thoughts made Kyan feel victorious. He'd been patient for years, and finally, he was about to see the fruits of his labor. He just had one final opponent before he could finally place the crown on his head.

Klax Turner.

As the time in the day winded down, an eager feeling crept in Kyan's stomach. He knew that by the fearful expression on Klax's face when he saw Kleigh that he would cooperate with all of his requests. The location of where Kyan kept Kleigh was the place he kept anything of value of his enemies. It was an old run-down building in Albany that had been many things before it was shut down. The last business that owned the property was a call center, which was why there was so much open space and random rooms to the side. In some rooms, there were things; in others, there were people. Sometimes in his business dealings, Kyan held things as collateral, whether it be an object or a person. And if the person doing business with him did not either pay what they owed or did as he asked them to, he kept whatever it was and did what he pleased with it.

He sat in what he had made his office in the back of the building. If a person sat inside and shut the door, it would be hard to believe how worn down the rest of the place was. He'd painted the walls, installed carpet, and had a custom-made desk imported from Tokyo. His fingers rasped the top of the mahogany desk as he contemplated the events of the night. His men had orders to shoot Klax the moment he introduced Kyan to the buyer, but not before he watched a bullet enter his sister's skull.

Knock! Knock!

"Come in," Kyan called out when he heard the knuckles against the wooden door.

"I brought her, boss," NuNu said and walked in with the young woman in tow.

Kyan's eyes didn't directly fall on her, but through his peripheral, he saw her sit down in the seat on the opposite side of the desk. Kyan's hand smoothed down the crisp green Versace button-up he wore as he glowered at NuNu who was having a hard time staring back.

"You good?" Kyan asked.

"Yeah, I'm straight," NuNu answered.

"You sure about that, because I've been hearing a pretty good story about you going around? You know what they're saying about you?"

"Nah, and I don't really care, either."

"Well, I care, because when niggas find you passed out in a whorehouse with your dick out, how do you think that makes you look? Weak. And how do you think that makes *me* look? Weaker than that," Kyan spoke in a frigid tone. "If it weren't for the fact that I'll need your impeccable aim tonight, I would shoot you where you stand."

"That dirty bitch drugged me," NuNu said. "Everybody done got played by some pussy before."

"You sound dumber than you look, little nigga!" Kyan barked. "If a bitch can get the one up on you, what message are you sending my enemies? Don't become a liability. I don't do liabilities. Go make sure everything is in place for tonight. We have a big move to make."

"You got it, boss," NuNu said sounding genuinely happy to have an out from Kyan's dangerous presence.

When he was gone, Kyan finally turned his attention to the young woman sitting across from him. She was pretty, although her eyes had a worn look about them. The clothes she had on were disheveled and dirty since she'd been wearing them for a few days. Her hair was messy, and a bath would have done her much good.

"Tell me something good, Cali," he said, and she jumped slightly when he said her name.

"I-I don't know what you mean, daddy," she spoke softly calling him what she used to call her pimp.

"You know exactly what I mean. I thought you were working on getting back into my good graces. You were supposed to befriend your new roommate."

"Oh, yeah. That."

"And what have you learned?"

Cali had been in his clutches for a little under a month when her pimp didn't want to pay what he owed. Eventually, he ended up paying with his life, and Kyan was going to do the same to Cali, but she had proven herself to be useful to him. That was, until she proved otherwise. While on a setup job with Joey Donald, a man who was 20K in the hole with Kyan, she decided to play with her nose. She got so high that she let it slip that people were coming to kill him, and he ran. It took a week for Kyan to finally catch up with him, and because of that slipup, she had to be punished. Her only option of redemption was to dive into the mind of her cell mate, Kleigh Turner.

"S-she's a tough cookie to crack, baby. She only talks about how she's sure her brother is gonna save her."

"Did she tell you anything else about her brother?"

"No. Nothing at all. Just that she knows he's gonna save her."

"Hmm, interesting," Kyan said, tapping his fingers on his desk.

It grew quiet in the room, and the only thing that could be heard were his fingers hitting the wood. He stared at her without blinking, searching her face for a lie. The only thing he found was fear.

"I'm telling you the truth, daddy," Cali said. "I wouldn't lie to you. I-I-I'm the one who told you the truth when I screwed up the last time."

"You're right," Kyan said, slowly reaching into his desk.

"I'll be a good girl," her voice came out as a plea. "I promise I won't mess up again."

"I know you won't . . . because you won't get the chance."

From his desk, he grabbed the .32 that he kept there and pointed it at her. Before she got a chance to move out of the way, he pulled the trigger. The gunshot was loud, and the bullet went through her throat and came out the back of her neck—a clean shot. Her eyes widened, and her breath turned into a gurgling sound. She wrapped her hands around her throat and tried to apply pressure to the wound, but it was futile. Kyan watched the life leave her within seconds, and she fell jerking to the ground until finally, she was still.

"I just got this damn carpet," Kyan complained.

It didn't matter, however, because, after that night, he would be switching locations permanently. He checked the diamond-studded watch on his wrist and saw that the time read almost four in the afternoon, and right on time, he felt his phone buzzing in his pocket. Sure enough, when he removed it and read the text message on the screen, it was an address from an unsaved number. It was showtime. He left the office, leaving Cali's body there to bleed out and headed over to the large parking garage where his people were waiting for him.

"You ready?" Kyan asked the large group of men as he approached the black Yukon trucks.

"Yes sir," they replied in unison.

"Then let's load up, boys! It's time to head out. This time tomorrow, we'll be on top of the world!" Kyan said, and they did as they were told.

Most of them were street soldiers, but a few of them were ex-military. If Klax had something up his sleeve, he still didn't have a chance against his manpower.

"The girl is in the van," NuNu said, walking up on Kyan and pointing to a white van behind the three trucks.

"Good, you ride with me," Kyan said, getting inside the back of a truck. "We both know I can't trust you around pretty girls."

The meeting place was in the Bronx, so Kyan reached the destination a little after six. It was an old loading warehouse so that they could pull their trucks into it with no problem. As promised, standing alone and unarmed next to an old freight was Klax. Kyan's goons, armed with automatic weapons, got out first to scope out the area. They fanned out while some went to check the back and the others went inside.

"Clear out back!"

"Clear inside!"

Once they heard that, NuNu got out and walked around to open Kyan's door for him. He stepped out and dusted the sleeves of his shirt before walking toward Klax. He had a smile on his face, while Klax looked somber. Beside and all around Kyan, all of his men had their weapons pointed at Klax just in case he tried something.

"Where's the buyer?" Kyan said, looking around. "I thought this was a meeting."

"Shit, you could have fooled me. Looks like you came in here prepared for war. How many people you got with you? I count twenty."

"Don't play with me, nigga. Where is he?" Kyan said, looking around. "You better not be gaming."

"He'll be here," Klax assured him. "But first, where is my sister? Before anything pops off, I need to see that Kleigh is still alive."

Kyan had half a mind to tell Klax to go to hell, but he told himself they would both be dead soon anyway. He nodded at NuNu, who went to the van and opened the back. From it, he pulled out a very alert Kleigh. Her wrists were bound, and her mouth was gagged, but she was still alive.

Kyan watched with satisfaction as the look of relief on Klax's face turned into one of malice. He chuckled and watched Klax's fists clench and release.

"You've seen what you needed to," Kyan said. "Now, it's time for you to hold up your end of the bargain."

"A'ight, I got you. You know how I just said he'd be here?"

"You mean he ain't coming?" Kyan said and put his hand up, preparing to give his goons the signal to blow Klax off his feet.

"Nah," Klax shook his head, and it seemed as if his tall frame suddenly got even taller. "He's already here."

Kyan looked around and waited to see somebody else enter the warehouse. When he didn't, he turned back to Klax, and that time, a broad smile came over his face. It took him a second, but Kyan finally understood what Klax meant.

"No. It can't be. The buyer is—"

"Me," Klax said with a short laugh.

"Nah," Kyan shook his head in disbelief. "You're lying. It can't be you. If you're the buyer, why run Harlem?"

"Harlem plays its part in the flow of New York," Klax told him. "I get the product, store it there, and distribute accordingly. I run marathons, not sprints, and there is always a bigger picture in my head. You hold the highest position on the board when everybody thinks you're playing the same game as them. I prefer to be an equally respected player on the surface, but in the background, I'm the one pulling the strings. Like right now."

"Right now?" Kyan scoffed. "Now that I know who you are, I have all the pieces on the board. You just gave yourself away to me. All for *her?*" He waved a disgusted hand at Kleigh. "You should have cut off your nose to spite your face because now, you've lost everything. Kill him!"

Pfft! Pfft! Pfft! Pfft! Pfft!

The shots were quick and precise. The five men closest to Kyan dropped to the ground with loud thuds as bullets lodged in their brains. On his right arm, Kyan noticed a red dot traveling in an upward motion to his chest and up to his face.

"It's on your forehead now," Klax confirmed when Kyan could no longer see it. "My people hung back until now. Now, you're all surrounded. One small move and you all die. Another mistake you made was assuming the fear of losing somebody I loved would make me sloppy. Nah. That made me sharp. It made me realize I was dealing with an amateur. You thought I would really come here alone? Why? Because I was desperate? I *was* desperate, and that's why you should have feared me. Tell 'em to drop their weapons before I redecorate this warehouse with *your* blood."

"Put them down," Kyan said, feeling the heat of the beam on his forehead.

"But, boss," Kyan heard NuNu say from behind him.

"Put your fucking weapons down!" Kyan shouted, and that time, they listened.

"Now, send my sister to me," Klax said.

Without turning around, Kyan motioned for NuNu to do as Klax said. Kleigh, who hadn't been given food or water since she'd been taken, stumbled past him, and he got a strong whiff of urine. When she got to Klax, he embraced her tightly as if he didn't smell a thing and kissed her forehead.

"You know I had you, right?" he said, ungagging her and freeing her wrists. "Who did this to your face?"

When she pointed back to NuNu, he pulled a pistol from the waist of his jeans. NuNu moved, knowing what was about to happen, but Klax was too fast for him. Since he moved, the bullet didn't explode his face like Klax wanted to, but it took off a large portion of his head. NuNu fell to the ground dead on impact, and Klax let the hand holding the gun fall to his side.

"Now, back to you," Klax said, looking back at Kyan. "You're lucky I'm in good spirits now that I have my sister back. I'm not gon' kill you."

"That ain't gon' be good for you, youngblood," Kyan snarled. "If I walk through them doors, best believe you won't make it to next week."

Dak dak dak dak dak dak!

Behind Kyan, the rest of the men he brought with him fell one by one as the automatic rounds tore into their bodies. When the gunshots stopped, Kyan stood like a lone soldier, and his eyes went from his people's dead bodies back to the mysterious smile on Klax's face.

"Oh, my bad, G. I guess I gave you the wrong impression," Klax said with a laugh. "I said, *I* wasn't gon' kill you. I *didn't* say you weren't gon' die."

That's when Kyan heard a voice that made his blood run cold.

"What's up, Unc?"

He barely had the chance to face the person he'd helped raise into a man when he heard two shots and felt heat explode in his chest. The last thing Kyan remembered was falling to the ground and seeing Tron's face staring emotionlessly down at him. He'd never felt pain like the one he felt right then as his blood seeped out of his body and onto the cold concrete underneath him. And then . . . nothing.

Chapter 21

"The question isn't who is going to let me; it's who is going to stop me?"

—Ayn Rand

Klax

Tron stood over Kyan with an AK-47 in one hand and a smoking pistol in the other. Klax thought he was going to empty the rest of his clip of the pistol in Kyan's body, but he didn't. He just watched him bleed out from the chest. Kyan's God complex had led him to a potential battlefield without a vest, and that was a fool's mistake. Tron's eyes stayed on Kyan's until all life left them, and *then* he emptied his clip into his face.

"Bitch," Tron said, breathing heavily. "That's for Sunny. My dad ain't deserve to go like that."

Klax, who was holding on to Kleigh for dear life, felt her try to pull away from him. He didn't want to let her go, but he knew somebody else needed her right then. She limped over to where Tron was, and he dropped the guns in his hands on the ground to catch her before she lost her balance. He embraced her as hard as he could without hurting her and buried his face in her neck.

"I'm sorry, shorty," he said to her. "This is all my fault."

"No. Don't say that. You came for me," she whispered weakly. "You both came for me. I love y'all so much."

Kyan was wrong about one thing. Tron might have lost his blood relatives, but he still had a family.

Klax's chest heaved up and down, and it wasn't until then that he realized how much relief he felt. He knew that the future held many more obstacles, but for right then, the worst was over. The way Tron held on to Kleigh let him know that he would probably be around for a while. After a few moments, Klax cleared his throat.

"Take her out of here," Klax told Tron. "I'm about to make a call to the cleaners and wait to make sure the job gets done right. There are more bodies than usual. I'll meet you back at her spot, bet?"

"Yeah," Tron said and lifted Kleigh with ease, placing an arm around her back and the other under her knees. He took a few steps toward the warehouse opening but stopped and turned back to Klax. "Aye, G?"

"What's good?"

"Thanks," was the only word that Tron could come up with to say.

"Ditto."

When Tron was finally gone, Klax heard the sound of someone climbing down from the warehouse's high ceiling. Klax wasn't alarmed because he knew who it was and offered a hand when the person landed on the high freight.

"You the only nigga that could ever ask me to get in the ceiling for anything!" Dame said, shaking his head at all the dead bodies around them. "That nigga really thought you had him surrounded."

"Shit, with the best shooter on my side, I see why it seemed like it!" Klax said and slapped hands with "You Dropped Five Niggas in Five Seconds Flat."

"You know, I just been working on my aim a li'l bit," Dame shrugged modestly. "But for real, anything for you and li'l sis. Y'all my people. I put that laser on his head and had him spooked, though, didn't I?"

The two men shared a laugh before Klax grew serious again.

"It ain't gon' stop with him, though," he shook his head. "Somebody gon' always want the crown."

"True. But that's something that comes with the job. Reason why you got niggas like me around you."

"True," Klax said with a sigh. "I'm growing tired of being two people. Now that y'all know my secret, I think it's time for me to pick a side."

"What does that mean?"

Instead of answering, Klax shrugged his shoulders. "Do me a favor."

"What's good?"

"Call the best cleaning team we have and stay here until the job is done."

"You ain't said shit but a word."

Tryn' to stay focus, kinda like Moses. Like somebody chose us . . ."

Nipsey's voice blessed Klax's ears, and he drove, nodding his head as if he hadn't just left a bloody crime scene. The entire ride to Kleigh's condo, Klax made peace with what had happened. He was thankful for the past because it helped him grow to be even better for the future. And when he was good mentally, everyone around him was too.

When he finally reached his destination, he stood outside the door for a few moments, listening to the voices on the other side. He found himself smiling when he heard Kleigh's laughter. He was worried that the experience might have traumatized her, but then again, he might have just underestimated the power of love. He'd spent so much time making sure no one could get close to her that he never thought about the weight it would take off his shoulders if she had someone solid in her corner. At first, he wasn't sure if it was Tron, but the way he gingerly had carried her out of the warehouse made him question that.

Knock! Knock!

His knuckles rasped against the door before he was yet ready to announce his presence, but he needed to speak to Tron. Kleigh swung the door open, and when she saw her brother, she hugged him tightly. She pulled away to look up in his face to examine him, and he did the same to her. She'd come home and cleaned up nice. His eyes went straight to her nose because with all the blood that had been there, he couldn't tell if it was broken the last time he saw her. When he was sure it wasn't, he kissed her forehead. She was still scraped and bruised, but that was just physical and would heal.

"What took you so long to get here?" she asked and eyed him worriedly. "Dame called Tron and said that everything is everything. He said you weren't answering your phone, though. You good?"

"I'm as good as I can be for right now," he said and shook his head when she stepped out of the way for him to come inside. "Nah, I'ma let y'all do your thing for right now. I wanted to holler at Tron for a second, though."

"All right, let me go get him," Kleigh said and closed the door.

A few moments later, Tron stepped into the well lit hallway with Klax. He let the door shut softly behind him and gave Klax a head nod.

"What's good, G?"

"Shit, I just wanted to come chat with you for a moment before I go handle my last little bit of business."

"No doubt, what's the word? Dame said everything got taken care of. Those motherfuckas move quickly!"

"Yeah," Klax nodded. "I only have the best on my team, and that's why I'm here."

"For what? Tell me I finally earned the position you want me in?"

"Yeah, something like that. I came to tell you which territory is yours," Klax said and looked down the hallway.

"A'ight. Where you gon' place me? The Bronx? I don't see them Mexicans going for that, though."

"Nah, they wouldn't, and that's why I'm giving you Harlem," Klax said and looked back at Tron's shocked face.

"What?"

"You heard me."

"So, after all this, you gon' just *give* me Harlem?"

"Yup, you can have it," Klax said and shrugged. "Like you said, after all of this, I've put a lot into perspective. I haven't had the time to really enjoy life because I've been so busy being two people. I just wanna be one person, and I trust you to do right by Harlem. I did what I wanted with it. Now you can rule how you see fit."

"You trust me?" Tron asked like he didn't believe Klax.

"I mean, not *trust*. You have caused quite a bit of trouble in my life in a short amount of time," Klax said with a grin. "But I can tell by the way my sister looks at you that there must be some good in there somewhere. She's taught me a lot, and she doesn't even know it. She taught me that you can't possess people. You can just enjoy life together with them. And, well, bro, let's enjoy life."

"I feel that," Tron said, and the two men slapped hands, pulling each other in for a brief embrace. "But you know, since I have a direct link to the buyer, I need to be the only nigga in New York with the highest-grade product."

"You already know," Klax told him. "Well, I'ma get out of here. Let y'all do y'all thing and shit. I'ma hit you tomorrow."

"A'ight, wait. Klax?"

"Yup?"

"You got another crib, don't you? I heard about what happened to yours. You know my pop owned a complex if you need a place to lay your head. I can hook you up with a new ride too. Yours done seen the end of days."

"Nah, I got a few spots around town, and I can always get a new whip. I have something I need to do before I turn it in for the night. Near-death experiences put you in a different state of mind, you know?"

"Nah," Tron said with a grin. "But I'ma let you have that. I'll fuck with you later, bro."

Tron went back in the condo, and Klax went on his way. Handing Harlem over had been hard, but the next stop was going to be slightly more difficult. Mainly because he didn't know what he was going to say.

He drove for thirty minutes, and the whole time he practiced in his head what would sound good coming out of his mouth, but nothing seemed right. It wasn't until he found himself standing outside the door of a third-floor apartment with his fist raised, ready to knock, that he lost his nerve. He backed away from the door and started back toward the stairs. He was almost there when he heard a door open behind him.

"Klax?" the sweet voice of a woman said, and he turned around to face her.

"What's up, Jas?" he said, and she gave him a confused look.

"I thought I heard somebody out here. You OK?" Jasmine said, standing there in a T-shirt and pair of shorts that hugged the figure he used to love so much.

"Yeah, yeah," Klax cleared his throat and nodded. "I'm good. I actually came to check on you after what happened the other night."

"Aah, yeah," she said with a nod. "I'm good. I was a little shaken up at first, but I'll be all right. I mean, you saved me, after all."

"Yeah, I did, didn't I?"

Klax didn't know what else to say, and for a moment, the two of them stared at each other. She was beautiful, as usual. As he looked at her, he didn't know how he had let her just exist around him for so long without making her his again.

"How did you let me just pass you up all these years?"

"What?" she asked. Her widening eyes were followed by her rapidly rosy cheeks.

"I mean, you said you loved me the other night. You ain't never said that before. Why didn't you ever let me know?"

"Because I showed you. But you were too busy being Klax Turner to see," she said to him. "When you broke things off with me, I thought you didn't want me. So I just tried to let it go, but as you can see, I can't. But I never wanted to complicate the friendship I was able to build with you or Kleigh after that, especially since I work at the bakery."

"I broke shit off with you back then because my life was getting too crazy. I didn't want you to get hurt. But now . . ."

"But now what?" Jasmine said, unable to hide the hopeful tone in her voice.

"Now, I don't think it would be so complicated," he said and cleared his throat again. "I mean, if you want. We can go out sometime or some shit. Do something you like to do, you know? Start fresh."

Jas burst out laughing. "Klax, when was the last time you asked a girl on a date?"

"I don't know," he answered truthfully with a shrug. "I never had to, to be honest."

"Well, the wrong way to do it is to show up unannounced at her house at almost nine o'clock at night." Jasmine put her hands on her hips as if she had an attitude.

"My bad. I ain't mean to impose. I guess I'll head out then." He started down the stairs, but she called his name again. He stopped and turned back to her. There was a disappointed look in her eyes as she stared back at him.

"What's up?"

"So that's it then?" she said, stepping out into the hallway and walking toward him. "That's all you came here to say to me? After all this time?"

"Girl, stop playing with me," Klax said. "You know how I feel about you. That shit ain't never went away. You ain't seen me with anybody else, have you?"

"Then why is it so hard to say it?"

"That I love you? 'Cause you should already know that. But I apologize if I've ever done anything to make you question it."

"Like push me away?" She took a few more steps toward him but stopped when she was directly in front of him. "Or never say it? Which one?"

"I'm here now, ain't I?" Klax motioned his hands for effect. "And I love you, Jas. Some recent events have shown me that our time here is really borrowed. I don't want to keep living with the thought that I have time to do certain things. I want to live every day like it's my last. Starting with right now, with you. So, are you with it, or what?"

"Once again, it's obvious that you *never* asked a girl out before. I don't know what I ever saw in you." Jasmine had a small smile on her lips as she stared into his face.

"Come on, man, you know I'm the smoothest nigga you've ever met," Klax grinned and placed his hands on her hips.

"You might be right about that. But if we try this again, you can't just up and leave out of my life because you're scared, a'ight? If you're gonna fuck with me, fuck with me. That's all I ask."

"I got you."

She stared at him for a few more moments, and he noticed that the disappointment had left her eyes. They lit up like the moon, and there was a smile frozen on her lips. She was happy, and he planned to keep her that way.

"OK, then," she said and motioned to her apartment. "I was just inside watching a movie. Do you want to join me?"

"Yeah," Klax said a little too fast and then laughed at his eagerness. "I mean, yeah, shorty. That sounds good."

"I thought you'd say that," she said, taking his hand.

She led him to her apartment, and Klax felt a multitude of emotions swarm over him. Lately, fate had been doing a lot of talking in his life, and when he began thinking about his life, his thoughts fell to Jas. His reasons for not being with her just didn't make sense anymore. He thought about how he would never know how far they could really go unless he tried. The lifestyle he lived, Klax knew he was either going to leave the world one or two ways. Before he left, he didn't want to have any what-ifs. He wanted happiness. And so far, on his happy list, he had crossed off almost everything. As he walked into Jas's apartment with her, he smiled to himself knowing that she was the last thing on that list. He smiled because his sister was home safe, he smiled because he'd gained a new friend, and he smiled because his future held endless possibilities.

The End

About the Author

C. N. Phillips was born and raised in Omaha, Nebraska, and harnessed her love for literature at the ripe ole age of 8. When she's not creating worlds, some of her favorite things to do are to travel, spend time with her family, and watch her favorite television show *Supernatural*.

To keep up with C. N., like her on:

Facebook at C. N. Phillips

Follow her other social media handles,

Twitter: @CNPhillips_

Instagram: AuthorCNPhillips.